Selected Writings of
Cunninghame Graham

Selected Writings

of

Cunninghame Graham

Edited by Cedric Watts

Rutherford • Madison • Teaneck
Fairleigh Dickinson University Press
London and Toronto: Associated University Presses

Associated University Presses, Inc.
4 Cornwall Drive
East Brunswick, N.J. 08816

Associated University Presses Ltd
69 Fleet Street
London EC4Y 1EU, England

Associated University Presses
Toronto M5E 1A7, Canada

Library of Congress Cataloging in Publication Data

Cunninghame Graham, R. B. (Robert Bontine), 1852–
1936.
Selected writings of Cunninghame Graham.

Bibliography: p.
I. Watts, Cedric Thomas. II. Title.
PR6013.R19A6   1981   828'.01200   00-70082
ISBN 0-8386-3087-1   AACR2

Printed in the United States of America

Contents

Part IV: Caudal

Selected Writings of
Cunninghame Graham

Part I
Preface

Biographical

Nothing could prevent Balfour being Prime Minister . . .; but Cunninghame Graham achieved the adventure of being Cunninghame Graham.

G. K. Chesterton: *Autobiography*

Robert Bontine Cunninghame Graham was born in 1852 and died in 1936; in the interim he became a celebrity, a notoriety, a living legend; and in the aftermath he has become, gradually, a forgotten figure, his achievements neglected. Those achievements were many, the most notable (as John Lavery[1] observed) being "his masterpiece—himself." He was a colourful, swaggering, protean adventurer: journalists called him "a cowboy dandy," "the Uncrowned King of Scotland," "the modern Don Quixote." He was variously traveller, cattle-rancher and horse-dealer, sword-fencer, Liberal M.P., pioneer Socialist, demagogue, convict, Mohammed el Fasi of Morocco, prospector for gold, begetter of Sergius Saranoff in Shaw's *Arms and the Man,* political columnist, essayist, critic, story-writer, historian, biographer, translator, leader of the Scottish Nationalists, "the curly darling" to factory

11

girls, and an expert with the lasso and with pistols. The list of his friends and acquaintances reads like a bizarre *Who's Who*. On political platforms he campaigned alongside William Morris, Friedrich Engels, Prince Kropotkin, Keir Hardie, H. M. Hyndman, Ben Tillett, Jim Larkin, Eric Linklater and Hugh MacDiarmid; he was admired by figures as diverse as Wyndham Lewis, George Bernard Shaw, Jacob Epstein, G. K. Chesterton, Ezra Pound and Theodore Roosevelt; his correspondents included H. G. Wells, Henry James, Thomas Hardy, Oscar Wilde, Lawrence of Arabia and John Galsworthy; and his closest literary friendships were with Joseph Conrad, W. H. Hudson and Edward Garnett.

He was born into the Scottish landed gentry as the heir to the large estate of Gartmore in Perthshire; his ancestry was three-quarters Scottish, one-quarter Spanish. On his father's side, he could trace his descent from Robert the Bruce, King Robert I of Scotland; another ancestor had fought and died beside William Wallace in 1298; and his family were claimants to the Earldoms of Glencairn, Strathearn, Menteith and Airth.

He was educated at Harrow and in Brussels, and at the age of seventeen went to South America to seek his fortune. During the subsequent years he frequently travelled in Central and South America, living among gauchos, llaneros and cattle-ranchers, making repeated attempts to prosper as a cattle- and horse-dealer—attempts which failed partly because of his youthful rashness, and partly because of Indian raids and the revolutionary upheavals in those regions. He married in 1878, and his young wife Gabriela (herself an artist with water-colours and pen) accompanied him on various arduous journeys including a trek from San Antonio (Texas) to Mexico City through territory raided by Indians.

Back in Scotland, after his father's death Robert struggled to manage the estate of Gartmore, which was heavily encumbered by debts (and which eventually had to be sold, though he himself remained a wealthy man). Soon, however, following a family tradition, he was attracted by radical politics. He was elected to Parliament as Liberal member for North-West Lanark in July 1886 and remained an M.P. until 1892. His Liberalism was nominal: he was attentive to the left-wing ideas of H. M. Hyndman and William Morris; the *People's Press* (26 April 1890, p. 3) regarded him as "the only member of Parliament who can really be called a Socialist"; and indeed he was in practice the first Socialist in the House of Commons—as his maiden speech suggests (see part II, "Political Polemics").

That speech was a dramatic success which helped to establish Graham as a national celebrity or notoriety. A contemporary observer wrote of it:

Advent of new man. Name: Cunninghame Graham. Description: Scotch Home Rule Visionary. Outward aspect: Something between Grosvenor Gallery aesthete and waiter in Swiss café. Person of "cultchaw," evidently, from tips of taper fingers to loftiest curl of billowy hair, and with sad, mournful voice to match. Drawls out some deuced smart things. Effect of speech heightened by air of chastened melancholy. House kept in continuous roar for more than half an hour. Fogeys and fossils eye him askance, and whisper that he ought to be "put down"; but lovers of originality, in all quarters, hail him with satisfaction. . . . Memorandum: To make a point of being present whenever Graham obliges. (*Vanity Fair*, 5 February 1887, p. 87)

That scornfully ironic and uncompromising maiden speech set the tone for his subsequent parliamentary appearances, during which he condemned British imperialism, profiteering landlords and industrialists, child labour, corporal and capital punishment, the House of

Lords, and religious instruction for school-children; and he advocated the eight-hour working day "in all trades and occupations," free education, Home Rule for Ireland and Scotland, and nationalisation of mining and industry generally. He was a lonely, challenging figure: on more than one occasion he was ordered by the Speaker to withdraw, and his retort—"I never withdraw!"—echoes whenever *Arms and the Man* is performed.

His notoriety increased with his part in the "Bloody Sunday" demonstrations of 13 November, 1887, when huge crowds of radicals, socialists, and workmen were involved in fights with police at Trafalgar Square and were not scattered until the Grenadier Guards appeared on the scene with fixed bayonets. Graham, arrested after a rush at the police, was subsequently found guilty of "unlawful assembly" and was sentenced to six weeks' imprisonment at Pentonville. His experiences as a convict did nothing to diminish his campaigning ardour: in 1888 he helped to found the Scottish Labour Party, becoming its President, with Keir Hardie as Secretary. At demonstrations on behalf of the dockers and of the campaign for the eight-hour day he appeared alongside Kropotkin, Engels, H. M. Hyndman and John Burns, and he travelled to Paris with Hardie and William Morris to speak at the Marxist Congress of the Second International. In 1892 his time in Parliament ended when he stood unsuccessfully as a Labour candidate.

After 1900, as the Labour group in Parliament gathered strength, he turned increasingly against it: he felt that once Labour Members arrived there, they became too "respectable," too eager to compromise. "I tell them . . . that they would do more good if they came to the House in a body drunk and tumbling about on the floor."[2] He continued to campaign on left-wing platforms but became increasingly the champion of extreme militancy, his rhetoric approaching advocacy of violent revolution. Indeed, in the period 1910–1914 there were many who considered violent revolution to be a real possibility in Britain. Among these was Winston Churchill, who as Home Secretary in 1911 imposed martial law, dividing the country into military districts in response to increasingly militant action by workers. It was a time of strikes, rioting and arson; during the street-battles between strikers and troops, many people were wounded and some died. Graham's fellow-speakers at this time were some of the most bitter and uncompromising orators of the day: Tom Mann, Ben Tillett, H. M. Hyndman and Jim Larkin.

The First World War ended this phase of social unrest. Graham had opposed Britain's entry into the conflict, but once Britain was committed to war with Germany the fact that he was officially too old for military service did not deter him from volunteering; and eventually he was given a War Office commission to work for the Army by purchasing in South America the horses to be used on the battlefields of France and Belgium.

After the war, in his later years he turned increasingly to the cause of Scottish Home Rule. He had long been its advocate; gradually it engrossed his campaigning energies. He became President of the National Party of Scotland and of its successor, the Scottish National Party, and was still head of the movement when he died in 1936.

There were good reasons why, in his lifetime, he had become known as "the modern Don Quixote." He had the style and swagger of a Spanish grandee; he admired Cervantes's hero, and on horseback, with his lean erect bearing, his upswept hair and his pointed beard, he bore some resemblance to Quixote; and his friends affectionately addressed him as Don Roberto. It is also the case that in his chivalrous impetuosity, in his concern for the underdog, and in his contempt for so much that passed for

modern progress he could be seen as quixotically anachronistic. Yet this "champion of lost causes" was also ahead
of his times. Many of the causes for which he fought so
zealously were eventually to succeed, or to have a substantial measure of recognition. They included, as we have
seen, the eight-hour working day, militant trade unionism,
the end of sweated labour, the emergence of a Labour
Party and free education; he championed the cause of
feminist emancipation from the 1890s onward, and urged
greater concern for oppressed racial minorities. Indignation against imperialism, which during the heyday of the
British Empire appeared so heterodox in him, has since
become a current orthodoxy. Even Scottish Nationalism,
which for so long was regarded by many Englishmen as an
eccentricity rather than as a political reality, showed in the
1970s that it could sometimes be a crucial force in British
politics. So perhaps one day Graham's foresight will gain
its due recognition.

His political career was only one of several. Another was
his career as a traveller, globe-trotter, and adventurer
abroad. He who had spent so many early years among
gauchos and llaneros in South America, heading for the
Andoo in onc ycai and crossing the Rio Grande in another,
had also travelled in Iceland, was an authority on Spain,
and had been an intrepid adventurer in North Africa. His
journey in Morocco, the quest for the city of Tarudant
(during which he travelled in the guise of Sheikh
Mohammed el Fasi, a sherif or holy man), was to be
recorded with irony and vividness in his volume *Mogreb-
el-Acksa*. Furthermore, notwithstanding his avowed contempt for "material interests," he was sufficiently aroused
by a passage in Pliny's *Historia Naturalis* to search for gold
at the site of a Roman mine-working in Spain, just as he was
to intrigue vainly for trading concessions in the Spanish
Sahara. Although such ventures failed financially, he prof-

ited by them artistically in his third career—his career as a writer, to which we now turn.

Notes

1. John Lavery, *The Life of a Painter* (Cassell, 1940), p. 92.
2. Quoted in W. S. Blunt, *My Diaries*, pt. 2 (London: Secker, 1920), p. 197.

Critical

Taken together, Parts II and III of this book illustrate one of the most interesting paradoxes of Cunninghame Graham: he was an activist in a hurry to change the world, yet he was also a thinker keenly aware of the impotence of all reforming activities when measured against the perennial force of death, decay, oblivion and human myopia. In his political writings he argued tirelessly on behalf of the underdogs whether they were the Africans, the chainmakers of Cradley Heath, the unemployed, the American Indians or nations denied autonomy, while his more literary works express a sceptical, pessimistic, even elegiac reflectiveness.

His polemical articles appeared in an extraordinarily wide range of magazines and newspapers, among them Keir Hardie's *Labour Leader,* H. M. Hyndman's *Justice* and *The Social-Democrat, The People's Press, The Glasgow Herald* and Frank Harris's *Saturday Review.* The articles were particularly numerous in the 1890s but continued to appear to the very end of his life, supported by his many letters to the press and interviews with reporters; sometimes he reported his own public appearances on the platform. One does not expect literary merit from political polemicists, but anyone who studies the newspapers and journals of those times will find that Graham's contributions tend to stand out from the mass of ephemera in which they appear. They have a lively lucidity, a pungency, an ironic and quirky vigour of expression; they may not be polished, the grammar and syntax may be faulty, but the voice is shrewd and clear, and it makes the struggles and injustices of yesteryear seem as vivid as today's. He was better at protests than programmes, better at voicing indignation and contempt than at formulating in detail some course of reform. But like that of Ruskin, Carlyle and Dickens, his rhetoric—slighter than theirs, yet engaging—is fearless in moving from the particular instance of injustice to the general indictment of modern industrial civilisation. He was a vigorous spokesman in a great radical tradition.

He was also, it may be said, something of an existentialist. More precisely, he was pyrrhonistic: radically sceptical, even about scepticism itself. He committed himself to certain moral and political causes because he felt they were right but not because he thought they would succeed. To Edward Garnett he once remarked:

> "Politics" you say. Yes, writing on politics is rot. But politics themselves are good, in this way. A man spends all his life for an idea (I speak of your Parnells etc), is spat upon, reviled, and laughed at for a fool, dies broken-hearted, hated by those he fought against, half understood (at most) by those he strove for, and most likely not thoroughly believing in the cause, for which he gave up his life.
> The last is the thing, and politics *that way* understood leaves literature, millions of leagues behind, even from an artistic standpoint.[1]

The romantic pessimism of this letter is actually a recurrent refrain in his literary works. Many of these he termed "sketches": a usefully vague generic term which embraces short pieces of considerable variety. Some are fictional tales; others are autobiographical reminiscences; still others are character-studies, reflective essays, travelogues and elegiac obituaries. In his lifetime, Graham saw the publication of seventeen volumes of such sketches, from *Father Archangel of Scotland* (1896) to *Mirages* (1936), in addition to four booklets containing single items. Besides these, his works include a guide-book (*Notes on the District of Menteith*, 1895), two travel books (*Mogreb-el-Acksa*, 1898, and *Cartagena and the Banks of the Sinú*, 1920), seven histories of the Spanish Conquest of South and Central America (from *A Vanished Arcadia*, 1901, to *The Horses of the Conquest*, 1930), and four biographies, of which the best is probably *A Braziliam Mystic* (1920). He published a translation from Gustavo Barroso and numerous prefaces (I have seen more than forty-five) to works by other writers. He also made a translation of Santiago Rusiñol's play, *La Verge del Mar*. Although never published, by some fluke of literary survival the play, in his translation (*The Madonna of the Sea*), was performed at Norwich twenty-two years after his death.

Just as Graham's political career has received inadequate attention from historians, who at best seem to present him as a picturesque supernumerary flitting at the fringe of the Labour movement, so Graham's literary work seems today to have been forgotten by the general public and the academic critics alike. Yet, in his lifetime, he was regarded as a master. He enjoyed distinct prestige as a writer, and, though his attitudes antagonised some readers, his works were customarily reviewed in tones ranging from the respectful to the gleeful. He impressed authors as diverse as Edward Garnett, Ezra Pound, Arthur Symons and John Galsworthy, while in 1931 Ford Madox Ford even claimed that Graham was "all in all, the most brilliant writer of that or of our present day."[2] Joseph Conrad's tributes, in his correspondence with Graham (his closest literary friend for many years), are generous almost to the point of sycophancy:

> My artistic assent [,] the intellectual and moral satisfaction with the truth and force of your thought living in your prose is unbounded without reservation and qualification . . . I don't know whether *Sketches* is the right name. As a matter of fact a new name should be invented for the form of the gems you have given to our literature. They are revelations of the uncommon in feeling and expression . . . Your quality so distinct in effect is in its essence elusive. It is not a superficial gift of brilliance, of wit, or picturesque phrase. It can't be reached by the critical finger because it lies deep. Its origin rests in the "sens profond de la vie" characterised by irony that is gentle and by a fierce sympathy.[3]

Frank Harris called Graham "an amateur of genius,"[4] and the fastidious reader of today may choose to underline that word "amateur." Graham was sometimes hasty and haphazard in style, and his tales may progress erratically, deflected by asides and digressions. He wrote hundreds of short pieces, and there may be an effect of repetitiveness if one reads too many at a sitting: the nostalgic traveller's anecdote, the elegiac obituary study, the fleeting incident at a lonely outpost, the character-sketch of a Spaniard, a Scot, or a whore—these subjects recur, and so do the wistful, melancholy moods. Nor was there much development between the early and the later writings, though they spanned over forty years. The early sketches are relatively erratic, jerky and bold, the later ones smoother and more reliably proficient, but there is not a great difference in merit between the periods.

Nevertheless, his work can still offer many pleasures. Even when he is not writing at his best, he is distinctive, original, provocative. The texture may be thin, but it is wiry; the descriptions may resemble cluttered catalogues, but he always has an eye for telling detail. As Paul Bloomfield has remarked, "Even when he makes his worst hash we can still taste the slice of life that went into the pot."[5] He records with relish the idiosyncratic and absurd, the inconsequentialities and irrationalities of life. And at his best he can be a morally provocative and technically striking writer. One reason for the neglect of his works is perhaps that they—sometimes deliberately, and with artful artlessness—defy categorisation: they raise unfamiliar problems for the critic and the general reader. A sketch that begins as a general essay on some philosophical or political theme will suddenly crystallize into a short, sharp, ironic anecdote; a travelogue will terminate in a precise vivid exchange of dialogue; a tale which seemed at first to be merely a character-sketch turns into an illustration of the paradoxes of memory or the hypocrisies of civilisation. This elusiveness is one of the qualities which at first puzzle but can eventually gratify the reader. "There is no dog-show for mongrels, alas," Laurence Davies once remarked to me; but if there were, he added, Graham's tales—those tousled literary mongrels—would carry away many prizes. Graham has been compared with Maupassant and Turgenev; more erratic and clumsy than either, he can sometimes bring the reader closer to the texture of individual human life than both. And he does so because of the closeness of his art to his experience. His tales form an extended and complex autobiography; and though it is the autobiography of a man who had a large stock of vanity and egotism, we also learn of a man who had magnanimous sympathies and indignations, and a capacity to see human efforts in multiple perspectives—sometimes contemptuous, sometimes pitying, but always interested and determined to rescue from oblivion the sights, sounds and encounters of a vanishing past.

Notes

1. Cedric Watts and Laurence Davies, *Cunninghame Graham: A Critical Biography* (London: Cambridge, 1979), pp. 290–91.
2. Ford Madox Ford, *Return to Yesterday* (London: Gollancz, 1931), p. 39.
3. *Joseph Conrad's Letters to R. B. Cunninghame Graham*, ed. Cedric T. Watts (London: Cambridge, 1969), pp. 160, 167.
4. *Contemporary Portraits (3rd Series)* (New York: Harris, 1920), p. 55.
5. *The Essential R. B. Cunninghame Graham*, ed. Paul Bloomfield (London: Cape, 1952), p. 17.

Editorial Note

With the obvious exception of Graham's maiden speech in Parliament (from *Hansard*), all the material in Part II first appeared in magazines. " 'Bloody Niggers' " subsequently reappeared in several anthologies, and "Bloody Sunday" was reprinted (in *New Age*) in 1908; but the remaining items have not been reprinted until now. For the material of Part III, I have used the text of the first publication in book form rather than of any previous publication in magazines, as Graham would generally have had greater opportunity to correct the proofs for a book than for a periodical. In both these parts I have eliminated obvious misprints, corrected the accentuation and reduced inconsistencies of typographic convention; and on a few occasions where the punctuation confused the sense, the punctuation too has been amended. Direct speech has been restored to the first item of Part II. Otherwise the texts remain in their pristine form, and in their entirety: there have been no elisions. Footnotes marked "C. G." are Graham's; all others are mine.

Like all anthologists, I have had to make a compromise between selecting the representative and the meritorious. My compromise gives rather more emphasis to the latter, though the merits are of various kinds. I have confined the selection to political essays and literary sketches, which can be reproduced in their entirety, and I have resisted the temptation to include extracts from the long works—the biographies, histories and travel books. This was partly because of considerations of space, and partly because it is a suspect operation to extract from their larger context short passages (however much they may resemble cameos). What I hope is that the selection that follows will lead the reader to explore later, and at leisure, the full diversity of Graham's works.

For permission to quote copyright material, I am grateful to Lady Polwarth and Mr. Andrew Hewson, the literary executors of R. B. Cunninghame Graham.

Part II
Political Polemics

Introduction

Graham's political campaigns were so many and various that the following selection represents only a tiny fraction of them; but it will give a clear idea of his particular kind of lively militancy.

Appropriately, the first item is his maiden speech as an M. P., delivered on 1 February 1887. The text is that of *Hansard's Parliamentary Debates* (Third Series, vol. 310, columns 441–45); but in the interests of immediacy I have taken the liberty of restoring to direct speech the words which *Hansard* conventionally renders in reported form. Graham's calculated effrontery and uncompromising radicalism are loud and clear; though he had entered the House as a Liberal, his peroration is markedly socialistic. When one reflects that this speech was offered in the year of Queen Victoria's Golden Jubilee, and over a decade before the Boer War, its boldness and verve seem particularly remarkable. This is wiry oratory—and the wire is barbed: barbed by irony and sly analogies; and there is a distinctive stylish tang. As in his literary works, Graham is fond of the archaic phrase, an echo of Elizabethan prose perhaps, and on the unexpected literary quotation from, say, Shakespeare or Pope, as well as of a pithily idiomatic directness.

The second piece, "Bloody Sunday," was written for William Morris's *The Commonweal* (10 November 1888, p. 354). Graham looks back on that turbulent "Battle of Trafalgar Square" in which, a year previously, he had been overpowered by the police, and writes with predictable bitterness and scorn of the methods used by the authorities against the demonstrators. Later, in *News from Nowhere*, Chapter 17, William Morris was to mythologize this battle as the start of the insurrection which toppled capitalism and inaugurated the Socialist Commonwealth in Britain.

Graham had seen at close quarters the misery and servitude of whole communities doomed to hopeless drudgery from childhood to death; and in "A Plea for the Chainmakers" (first published as part of a penny pamphlet entitled *The Nail and Chainmakers,* 1889) he describes the horrors of Cradley Heath, near Birmingham, and makes detailed proposals for reform. Though elsewhere he expressed more revolutionary views, he knew that it would be callous not to strive also for immediate reform at places like Cradley. The picture he paints is almost Dickensian in its grim vividness; and the humanity, too, finds a Dickensian eloquence at times in this piece—particularly when Graham is condemning those who by bland abstract phrases about "the laws of supply and demand" would veil from themselves and others the stark actuality of suffering men and women.

" 'Bloody Niggers' " appeared in H. M. Hyndman's *The Social-Democrat* for April 1897, (vol. 1, pp. 104–9), and soon became the most famous of Graham's polemical pieces: it was republished under the bowdlerised title "Niggers" in several later collections. It exemplifies Graham's oblique approach to a topic, by indirections finding directions out. The object of his attack is imperialism generally, but more particularly the British imperialism preached by the political Darwinians, who claimed that it was nature's law—and doubtless God's law too—that Britain should display her fitness for survival, by competing with other European powers for the right to conquer as much of the globe as possible. Instead of proceeding directly to his attack on exploitation in the name of Empire, Graham begins, partly tongue-in-cheek and partly in earnest, with a vast panorama of the splendours and diversity of the creation, before leading a wildly impetuous charge against the barbarism and cruelty of imperialism.

He opposed exploitation wherever he saw it, whether it was of race by race, of class by class, or of sex by sex. As early as the 1890s—long before the term "suffragette" came into common use—he had spoken on behalf of feminist emancipation. Of his writings on this theme I have chosen "The Real Equality of the Sexes" (from *The New Age*, 11 July 1908, p. 207), as it shows that even in 1908 his position was well in advance of contemporaneous "progressive thought." Graham points out in this piece that even when women succeed in obtaining the vote, and even if they succeed in obtaining economic equality with men, their position will be little changed unless there is a moral and sexual revolution which will give the woman as much personal liberty as the man.

Other political radicals become mellow as they age; Graham, in the period 1906–1914, became more bitterly extreme. Never more bitter, perhaps, than when he attended the Trades Union Congress at Newcastle in 1911 and found that the Union leaders, instead of denouncing Winston Churchill's strike-breaking military régime, were content to follow the path of quiet moderation. His violent impatience and near-desperation are recorded in "Il Gran Rifiuto" (*Justice*, 23 September 1911, p. 4); and in "The Enemy" (*Justice*, 3 May 1913, p. 5) his socialism reaches an anarchistic extreme:

Enemies of the present state of things must be enemies not only of the State and all its works, political and economical, but of the Churches and their moralities and faiths. There is no other halting-place for Socialists.

The final phase of his career, when Scottish Nationalism came to dominate his political thoughts, is represented by the speech reported under the heading "Scotland's Day: 21st June 1930" in *Scots Independent* (July 1931, Supp. pp. 2–6). To the last, there was a central consistency about his apparently erratic career, for even in the 1880s he had been dedicated to Home Rule for Ireland and Scotland, and the cause was part of his perennial concern for the world's underdogs. Scots may note, however, that he once defined their Nationalist cause as the right of the people to see their taxes wasted in Edinburgh instead of in London. This blend of the idealist and the realist, the romantic and the cynic, is characteristic of Cunninghame Graham's paradoxial genius.

Maiden Speech

A debate on the Queen's Speech forms the best occasion for a new Member to lose his political virginity, and, therefore, I cast myself at once on the forbearance and generosity of the House.

On glancing over the Queen's Speech, I am struck with the evident desire which prevails in it to do nothing at all. There is a similarity in its paragraphs to the *laissez-faire* school of political economy. Not one word is said in the Speech about lightening the taxation under which Her Majesty's lieges at present suffer; not one word to make that taxation more bearable; not one word to bridge over the awful chasm existing between the poor and the rich; not one word of kindly sympathy for the sufferers from the present commercial and agricultural depression— nothing but platitudes, nothing but views of society through a little bit of pink glass. To read Her Majesty's Speech, one would think that at this present moment this happy country was passing through one of the most pronounced periods of commercial activity and prosperity it had ever known. One would think that wheat was selling at fifty shillings a quarter, and that the price of bread had not gone up. One would think that poverty, drunkenness, prostitution and wretchedness were in a fair way to be utterly extirpated; and one would think further that Great Britain had made the first important step towards that millennium when the Irish landlord would cease from troubling, and when the landlords and tenants would lie down in amity, and finally be at rest.

Of course, it is matter for congratulation that this country is not suddenly called upon to enter upon a quixotic crusade to place Prince Alexander of Battenberg upon the Throne of Bulgaria. We are thankful for small mercies, and I suppose we must be content. If this unhappy nation has to forego the pleasure of paying for the vagaries of Prince Alexander, it has still a pretty large group of needy Royalties who are placed on the Civil List of this country.

It was not to be expected that Her Majesty's Government would vouchsafe to the House any idea of when the British troops might be withdrawn from Egypt. That was expecting far too much. But, surely, it would have been wise to let the House know when it was intended to withdraw these troops from their inactivity in that pestilential region, and from playing the ungrateful *rôle* of oppressors of an already down-trodden nationality. But no. The bondholders must have their pound of flesh. We must also protect the so-called high road to India by the Suez Canal, in order that the very last straw may be laid on the unfortunate fellahin, and that British money and British treasure may be poured out like water. I have forgotten the "cent per cent." I have forgotten by whose advice we are in Egypt—that it was by the advice of that illustrious statesman and economist who has raised the art of carpet-bagging from its primitive rudeness into a political science, and who so well illustrates the Scriptural injunction, "When they persecute you in one city, flee to another."[1]

With reference to our latest filibustering exploit in

Burmah, it is a matter of great congratulation—it is
something on which a Christian may truly plume himself,
to hear that Her Majesty's Government are in process of
rapidly suppressing brigandage, which has grown up in
the country, and in putting down bands of marauders.
"Marauders," like "mobled Queen," is "good,"[2] very good,
when applied to poor, unfortunate, misguided people,
who, in their pig-headed way, are endeavouring to defend
their own country. Does the House recognize how a band
of marauders is put down? I do; I have seen it done often.
Surely, it can be no great matter of self-congratulation for
Britons with arms of precision to shoot down naked savages. It will be no feather in a soldier's cap to suppress
these unfortunate wretches with all the resources of civili-
zation at his command. When the telegrams come from
Burmah we slap our hands on our chests, quite regardless
of damage to our shirts, and talk of British gallantry; and
so we laugh like parrots at a bagpiper, when we look at the
sketches in the illustrated papers depicting Natives running away from our troops. A Native wounded to death, I
take it, and tormented by mosquitoes in the jungle, feels
his misery as acutely as the best be-broadclothed gentle-
man among us, even though he should happen to be a
chairman of a School Board; but what is all this to the
Government? The Government, like an American hog,
must root or die.

The question is, how did this Government come in? This
is the humour of it. They came in by the help of the
pseudo-Liberals—the crutch-and-toothpick Gentlemen—
through the assistance of that feeble Union ladder which,
having been used and abused, is now about to be cast
aside and kicked into the dunghill.[3] I was delighted to
see how the noble Lord (Lord Randolph Churchill) last
night treated his Unionist allies—to observe that, having
betrayed their master, like Judas Iscariot, there was but

one resource left for them, and that was to go out and hang themselves—and to see how these superior persons fell out and bespattered one another, and I thought to myself, "How these mugwumps love one another." The Government reminds me of Pope's flies in amber:

> Things in themselves though neither rich nor rare,
> One wonders how the devil they got there.[4]

Personally, I regret the resignation of the noble Lord the Member for South Paddington. He was a type in times of dull uniformity, and from the depth of my obscurity I admired the noble Lord's parabolic course. The noble Lord's resignation has saddened me as children are saddened when they see a rocket spout up and are all unaware that it will fall down a stick—as was well said by Ben Jonson:

> He was a child that so did thrive in grace and feature,
> As Heaven and Nature seemed to strive which owned the
> creature.[5]

Where is the noble Lord now? Yesterday he was, to-day he is not—gone like the froth on licensed victuallers' beer, or the foam on petroleum champagne, leaving Her Majesty's Government, alone and unaided, to wrestle with the difficulties of the situation, and to give "their careful consideration to all the matters" pertaining to their function.

With respect to Ireland, I have eminent qualifications for dealing with this subject, for many reasons. First of all, I have never been there; secondly, sitting next to Nationalist Members, I have gained, of late, something of a National colour; and I once knew an Irish commercial traveller, who imparted to me various facts quite unattainable by the general public. I have also gained much information from the Hon. Member for Cambourne (Mr. Conybeare), who has recently been staying with the nobility and gentry of that country. From these sources, I have conceived a warm respect and regard for that much-abused and down-trodden class—the Irish landlords, who are held in the deepest affection by their tenants. As to the Glenbeigh evictions,[6] the landlords have been held up to most unjust obloquy, as they have ever been most kind to their tenants, whom, in fact, they have kept in cotton wool. It is the pride and privilege of the Irish landlord to look after the interests, creature as well as spiritual, of his tenants; and, such is the relation of class to class that, so far from turning them out on a bleak, cold winter's night, the landlord has provided his dependents with a fire to warm their hands; only, through a pardonable inadvertence, it is their houses that furnish the blaze.

The Government has lighted a light that will serve to light the Liberals on their path. The homes destroyed in Glenbeigh were, no doubt, as dear to the poor peasant, in his lonely village on the stony mountain side in the far west, as is the shoddy mansion in South Kensington to the capitalist, as is Haddon Hall to its owner, or as is Buckingham Palace to the absentee owner of that dreadful building. Who can say that the affairs of this handful of obscure tenants in a wind-swept and rain-bedewed, stony corner of Ireland, may not prove to have given the first blow to this society in which one man works and another enjoys the fruit—this society in which capital and luxury make a Heaven for thirty thousand, and a Hell for thirty million—this society whose crowning achievement is this dreary waste of mud and stucco—with its misery, its want and destitution, its degradation, its prostitution, and its glaring social inequalities—the society which we call London—this society which, by a refinement of irony, has placed the mainspring of human action, almost the power of life and death, and the absolute power to pay labour and to reward honour, behind the grey tweed veil which enshrouds the greasy pocket-book of the capitalist.

Notes

1. Matt. 10:23. Sir Evelyn Baring had been the Government's adviser in India before becoming Consul-General of Egypt.

2. Graham mockingly links the term "marauders," from the Queen's Speech, with Polonius's " 'Mobled queen' is good" (Shakespeare, *Hamlet,* Act 2, scene 2).

3. The Conservative Government had been helped to power in 1886 by the division in the Liberal Party between the Gladstonians, who sought Home Rule for Ireland, and the Unionists, who opposed Home Rule. Lord Randolph Churchill, who had recently resigned from office as Chancellor of the Exchequer, had referred to the Unionists as a crutch to be thrown aside when the Government gained strength.

4. A version of lines 171–3 of Alexander Pope's "An Epistle . . . to Dr. Arbuthnot."

5. A version of lines 5–8 of Ben Jonson's "Epitaph on S.P., a Child of Queen Elizabeth's Chapel."

6. At Glenbeigh in County Kerry, poor tenants with long arrears of rent were being evicted; the bailiffs set fire to some of the cottages to prevent re-entry.

Bloody Sunday

(To the Editor of the *Commonweal*)

Except the facts already known to the public, I fear I can tell little of the occurrences in Trafalgar Square last November.[1] As to the reason why three men were killed, many sent to prison, three hundred or so arrested, and several condemned to penal servitude; the retail trade of the metropolis thrown into disorder, the troops called out; as to why men and *women* were beaten and brutalised in the public streets, the wherefore that the powers that be chose to expose their capital to the chance of being sacked and burnt by an angry populace,—I confess that I am still in the dark. The more I think, the more I cannot tell. It may be that Sir Charles Dogberry[2] had heard of, and wished to imitate, the behaviour of the negro pilot who came aboard a ship in the West Indies, and immediately gave the order, "Haul um jib up, Mr. Mate," and then, amidst the curses of the crew, instantly remarked, "Haul um jib down, Mr. Mate"; giving as his reason that he wished to show his authority.

What I can tell you is merely this, that I was in Birming-

ham and read in the morning papers that a meeting
having for its object to petition the Government for the
release of Mr. William O'Brien, M.P.,[3] had suddenly been
proclaimed without rhyme or reason. At that time I was a
newly elected Liberal member. I had heard members of
my party, men who at that time I respected and believed to
be in earnest, talking big at meetings and telling lies about
what they intended to do that autumn. I had read Mr.
Gladstone's speech at Nottingham, in which he had ex-
pressly said that coercion would not be confined to Ireland, but would also be applied to England if the people
were supine. I had read this, and—fool that I was—I
believed it; for at that time I did not know that Liberals,
Tories, and Unionists were three bands of thimbleriggers.
I did not know that the fooleries of Harcourt and the
platitudes of Morley were anything else than the utterances of dull good men, who at least believed in themselves.[4] I was soon to be undeceived.

To return to my meeting. I came up to London, hearing
that the meeting was held under the auspices of the
Radical clubs of London, in conjunction with the Irish
National League. Now one would have thought that I
should have met at every political club in London the local
Liberal member encouraging his constituents. One would
have thought that the boasters and braggers from the
county constituencies would have rushed up to town to
redeem their vaunts on public platforms. I expected that it
would be thought as cruel and tyrannical to break up a
meeting at which thousands of Irishmen were to be present, in London as it would be in Ireland. I thought that
freedom of speech and the right of public meeting were
facts in themselves, about which politicians were agreed. I
did not know the meanness of the whole crew even at that
time. I was not aware that freedom of speech and public
meeting were nothing to them but stalking-horses to hide

themselves behind, and under cover of which to crawl into Downing Street. I soon found, however, that the Liberal party was a complete cur, that what they excelled in doing was singing "Gloria Gladstone in excelsis," and talking of what they intended to do in Ireland. You see the sea divided them from Ireland, and one is always brave when no danger is at hand. However, no political capital was to be made out of London, it appeared, therefore Mr. Shaw-Lefevre[5] thought better to vapour and obtain a cheap notoriety in Ireland, where he knew he was quite safe, than to help his fellow townsmen—he is, I think, a Londoner—in London, where there might have been some incurred.

Finding myself deserted by all my colleagues, with the exception of Messrs. Conybeare and Walter McLaren, who would have been at the meeting had they been able, and at that time not knowing many of the Radicals, I turned to the Socialists, some of whom I did know, and hearing their procession was to arrive at St. Martin's Church at a certain time, I determined to join it.

What happened is known to all: how no procession reached the Square; how they were all illegally attacked and broken up, some of them miles from the Square; how in despite of every constitutional right, and without a shadow of pretext, banners and instruments were destroyed, and not a farthing of compensation ever given, though the loss fell on poor people. It will be remembered, too, how the police, acting under the orders of Sir Charles Dogberry, the Christian soldier *(sic)*, felled men and women, and in some cases little children, to the ground. I wonder if Mr. Henry Matthews, the pious Catholic Home Secretary, approved of this, and how he broached the matter to his priest when he went to confession? It will not be forgotten the sort of bloody assize that followed, and how Judge Edlin wrote himself down ass by the folly of his sentences. No one will forget the trial and condemnation of George Harrison,[6] and his sentence to five years penal servitude on the oath of one policeman, eleven independent witnesses being of no avail to save him. Then the pantomimic trial of John Burns and myself, and our condemnation by Mr. Justice Shallow,[7] also on the testimony of professional witnesses, and for an obsolete offence. It is still, I think, fresh in the memory of all, how with the help of all the professional perjurers in London, all the arms collected from that vast crowd amounted to three pokers, one piece of wood, and an oyster-knife. How I failed to join the procession, and having met Messrs. Burns and Hyndman by accident, proceeded to the Square; how we were assaulted and knocked about and sent to prison, is matter of notoriety in London.

I can tell no more of the incidents of that day than can any other spectator. I walked across the street with Burns, was joined by no one as far as I can remember, and found myself a prisoner in the Square with a broken head. Whilst in there though I had ample time to observe a good deal. I watched the crowd and the police pretty carefully; I saw repeated charges made at a perfectly unarmed and helpless crowd; I saw policemen not of their own accord, but under the express orders of their superiors, repeatedly strike women and children; I saw them invariably choose those for assault who seemed least able to retaliate. One incident struck me with considerable force and disgust. As I was being led out of the crowd a poor woman asked a police inspector (I think) or a sergeant if he had seen a child she had lost. His answer was to tell her she was a "damned whore," and to knock her down. I never till that time completely realised how utterly servile and cowardly an English crowd is. I venture to say that had it occurred in any other country in the world, the man would have been torn to pieces. But no! in England we are so completely accustomed to bow the knee before wealth and riches, to repeat to ourselves we are a free nation, that in the end we have got to believe it, and the grossest acts of injustice may be perpetrated under our very eyes, and we still slap our manly chests and congratulate ourselves that Britain is the home of Liberty.

Other things I saw that pleased me better than this. I saw that the police were afraid; I saw on more than one occasion that the officials had to strike their free British men to make them obey orders; I saw that the horses were clumsy and badly bitted, and of no use whatever in a stone street; and lastly, I am almost certain I observed several of the police officers to be armed with pistols, which I believe is against the law. I saw much too, to moralise on. The tops of the houses and hotels were crowded with well dressed women, who clapped their hands and cheered with delight when some miserable and half-starved working-man was knocked down and trodden under foot. This I saw as I stood on almost the identical spot where a few weeks ago the Government unveiled the statue of Gordon, not daring to pay honour to the memory of one of our greatest latter-day Englishmen because they feared the assembling of a crowd to do him honour; because, I suppose, for both political parties the comments on the death of a man sacrificed to their petty party broils would have seemed awkward. As I stood there, as I saw the gross over-fed faces at the club and hotel windows, as I heard the meretricious laughter of the Christian women at the housetops (it is a significant feature of the decadence of England, that not one woman of the upper classes raised her protest by pen or on platform to deprecate the treatment of her unarmed fellow-countrymen; no, all their pity was for the police), I thought yet, still—I have heard that these poor working-men, these Irishmen and Radicals have votes, and perhaps even souls, and it seemed impossible but that some day these poor deceived, beaten, down-trodden slaves would turn upon their oppressors and demand why they had made their England so hideous, why they ate and drank to repletion, and left nothing but work, starvation, kicks, and curses for their Christian brethren? Somewhat in this style I thought; this I saw as I stood wiping the blood out of my eyes in Trafalgar Square. What I did not see was entirely owing to the quietness of the crowd. I did not see houses burning; I did not hear pistols cracking. I did not see this—not because of any precautions the authorities had taken, for they had taken none, but because it was the first time such a scene had been witnessed in London during this generation.

Now, whilst thanking the *Commonweal* for giving me so much space, I can only say that I do not contemplate the renewal of such a scene with much pleasure. "You can beat a cow until she is mad," says the old proverb; and even a Londoner may turn at last. I hope that there may be no occasion for him to turn in my life-time, but I know that if he is not forced to do so he will have only himself to thank for having avoided it. No party will help him, no one cares for him; rich, nobles, City, West End, infidels, Turks, and Jews combine to cheat him, and he stands quiet as a tree, helpless as a sheep, bearing it all and paying for it all. This, then, is all I can tell of the great riots (*sic*) in Trafalgar Square, where three men were killed, three hundred kicked, wounded, and arrested, and which had no result, so far as I can see, but to make the Liberal party as odious and as despised as the Tory party in the metropolis. All honour to the Socialists for being the first body of Englishmen in the metropolis to have determined that the death of three Englishmen, killed by the folly of Sir Charles Dogberry, and worthy Mr. Verges, the Home Secretary,[8] shall not go unregarded, and I hope unpunished. I am, Sir, your obedient servant,

R. B. Cunninghame Graham.

Notes

1. On 13 November 1887, socialist and radical groups had proceeded towards Trafalgar Square on behalf of various causes including the rights of assembly and free speech, sympathy with William O'Brien and other Irish patriots, and the plight of the unemployed. The authorities had banned the demonstration there in the hope of averting a riot. The riot ensued as the demonstrators encountered the police and troops.

2. Here Graham unites the Chief Commissioner of Police (Sir Charles Warren) with Constable Dogberry of Shakespeare's *Much Ado about Nothing*.

3. William O'Brien had been jailed as an organiser of the Irish "Plan of Campaign" (a plan to withhold rents until reductions or rebates were granted).

4. Sir William Harcourt and Sir John Morley were prominent Liberals who supported the cause of Irish Home Rule.

5. Shaw-Lefevre was a Liberal M.P. who had advocated the establishment of an Irish Assembly to settle Irish affairs.

6. George Harrison had been charged with stabbing a policeman on Bloody Sunday.

7. Burns and Graham had been sentenced to prison for "unlawful assembly" by Mr. Justice Charles, whom Graham links with the senile Justice Shallow of *Henry IV*, Part Two. (Burns was a popular orator of the revolutionary Social-Democratic Federation, which was led by H. M. Hyndman.)

8. Graham equates the Home Secretary, Henry Matthews, with Shakespeare's Verges, who (like Dogberry) is a comic constable in *Much Ado about Nothing*.

A Plea for the Chainmakers

The condition of the people at Cradley Heath has been well known for the last fifty years to the public. Disraeli called it Hell-Hole. Royal Commissions not a few have reported on it. Radicals have questioned about it. Philanthropists have sighed and passed on. Clergymen of various denominations have passed lives of modest usefulness endeavouring to divert the minds of the people from the ills they endure in this world, to the prospective happiness they may enjoy in the next. But nothing has, so far as I am aware, ever been attempted in a practical way to improve their condition.

Royal Commissions, reports, etc., are excellent things in their way, but there is little use in them if they are not acted upon and merely serve to swell the pile of correspondence in the pigeon-holes of some office in Downing Street. Such is their general fate.

I have never gone to Cradley Heath without coming away in the lowest spirits. The mud is the blackest and most clinging, the roads the slushiest and ruttiest, the look of desolation the most appalling, of any place I have ever seen.

An able pamphlet[1] written some years ago, called
"Chains and Slavery," puts forth the condition of the
people better than I can. It would require a Zola to write
their epic, and a Millet to paint their outward semblance.
Still they would fail. An Englishman alone could, I think,
render their dumb protest into fitting words, and such an
Englishman has not yet been found.

Wages, it is said, have risen all over England. The
condition of the wage-earners has bettered ten-fold, say
the economists! It may be so, but what, then, must have
been the condition of the Cradley Heath chain-makers
fifty years ago?

Let me try to place before you Cradley Heath.

A long, straggling, poverty-stricken, red brick, Worces-
tershire village. Houses all aslant, with the subsidences of
the coal workings underneath. Houses! yes, houses, because people live in them. But such dens! Ill-ventilated,
squalid, insanitary, crowded; an air of listlessness hanging
on everything. Not a pig, not a chicken, not a dog to be
seen. A fit place in which to preach thrift, and economy,
and abstinence! Oh, yes, especially abstinence—but from
what?

Something picturesque withal about these wretched
houses, something old-world about the shops where the
people slave. Something of pre-machinery days in the
deliberate tenacity with which the chains are made. The
crowded little workshop, with its four or five "hearths," its
bellows, its anvils, its trough of black water, its miserable
baby cradled in a starch box. The pile of chains in the
corner, the fire of small coals, the thin, sweating girl, or
boy, or old man (every one seems either very young or
very old at Cradley, age seems to follow so hard on youth).
The roof without ceiling, the smell of bad drainage, the
fumes of reeking human beings pent in a close space—
such is a Cradley Heath workshop.

Mud, dirt, desolation, unpaved streets, filthy courts, narrow reeking alleys, thin unkempt women, listless men with open shirts showing their hairy chests. Mud, dirt; dirt and more mud—such is Cradley as regards its streets.

Work, work, always; ever increasing; badly paid; from early dawn till after dark; from childhood to old age, and this is the chain they forge. Stunted forms, flattened figures, sallow complexion, twisted legs from working the treadle hammer (Oliver), are the outward and visible signs of which the chain and nailmakers' dull, dogged, despairing resignation, born of apathy and hunger, is the inward and spiritual grace.

To sum up the position briefly. Failure of civilisation to humanise; failure of commercialism to procure a subsistence; failure of religion to console; failure of Parliament to intervene; failure of individual effort to help; failure of our whole social system.

But the time has come, the electric light of public opinion is turned for the moment upon Hell-Hole. What will it do? Merely flash off again, and leave the darkness more intense? Or will it bring life and health and hope?

I have little doubt there are many philanthropic people ready to help these poor folk if their case were widely known. Truly, they lack advancement, but not charity.

I have always contended that what is wanted at Cradley is the temporary advance of some portion of the wealth that the district has created. It should be remembered that very little small chain is made in any other part of England. It should be remembered that many profits, apart from the legitimate cost of distribution, are made off small chain before it reaches the consumer, and that if those profits remained with the producer no charity would be needed. All parties in the State alike condemn the middleman. Well, an opportunity has presented itself to get rid of him in this district. But not by praying, not by reading reports, or poring over statistics. Action! Action is what is wanted, and prompt action too.

What says Mr. Burnett's report in reference to the various Commissions, Reports, Select Committees, etc.? "The general drift of these reports and of the evidence is to the effect that for at least 150 years the condition of the nailors has been wretched in the extreme, except during brief seasons. . . ." Wretched during 150 years; during all the period of England's commercial supremacy; during the rise of the machine industry; whilst the steam engine was supplanting the stage coach; whilst discoveries to lighten labour (*sic*) were being made—during all this time these men were hammering away making nails, and were wretched, were starving, worse, I say, than savages, for in their distress savages see no wealth about them.

"It may be said," says Burnett, "that excepting the abatement [mark the word abatement, it should have been abolition] of the truck system and the excessive employment of children, all the evils then complained of as existing in the nail and chain trade exist to-day intensified to some extent by increased population and the pressure of outside competition, whether from abroad or increased application of machinery to the work of production." "Evils intensified!" a good reason, I suppose, to do nothing and to prate of not interfering with the course of trade; to twaddle about supply and demand, and so forth. I have no doubt that to some it may seem as foolish to throw doubt on the laws of supply and demand, etc., as on the law of gravitation, but whilst one is an established scientific fact—easily established by throwing a stone into the air—the other law is merely a rhapsody of words, merely a piece of defensive armour invented by fools who, in the main, knew nothing of what they wrote, and seized upon by knaves eager to strengthen themselves in the possession of their ill-gotten gains.

And all this has been known for years. Liberals and Tories alike have known it, and have done nothing. Nothing has been done, or will be done, I fear, whilst the bulk of both parties are rich men and employers of labour. Anyhow, the present state of this district is a scandal to both parties, a satire on civilisation, and makes one doubt whether Parliament, as we now know it, with its stupid fuss, its stupid men, and its foolish measures, is of any advantage to the poor at all.

But there is a greater power than Parliament; there is the power that made Parliament and can unmake it; the power that pays for the green covered seats, the Speaker's wig, the mace and all the other baubles; and if Parliament is deaf, the masters of Parliament—the people of England—will, if they read this dull pamphlet, at least be able to judge of the true state of the case. Perhaps the way to put things best before them is to quote from Mr. Burnett's report:

Harrison, aged 53, and his daughter Eliza, 28 . . . work in a dark little shop in a most insanitary and filthy court . . . making nails . . . had to work late and early to earn 15s. per week between them out of which they had to pay 2s. for breeze (small coal)   family of seven . . . lived mostly on tea, and bread and bacon. On Sundays they might be able to get a morsel of meat, or "beef cheek," to boil and make soup with . . . Eliza enumerates as chief items of expenditure: two ¼ lbs. of tea at 6d., 4 lbs. of sugar at 2d., meat 3s. to 3s. 6d., 1s. 10d. for coals, 2s. for house rent, and 1s. 6d. for bacon.

No fear, I should think, of pauperising these people by helping them; little chance of undermining their self-reliance, so dear to Englishmen (rich ones).

Joseph Marson, 83 . . . had been 75 years a nailor . . . nails he had known at 2s. a bundle now only 8d. . . .

could earn 2s. 6d. a week when he could get nails to make, and got 2s. 6d. a week from the parish.

Five shillings a week is generous pay at 83, after a life of toil. Still, God forbid that we should interfere with the course of trade. The weakest to the wall, my worthies. You see this old man was the victim of an "economic pressure," therefore let us bow down before "economic pressures" when they do not touch ourselves. Let us, if we be Tory Pharisees, talk of the greatness of the Empire—it appears that the shop where he worked for 75 years was all the empire Citizen Marson knew. If we be Liberal Publicans, let us refuse to interfere with supply and demand. In either case, Joseph Marson will soon be in his pauper's coffin and will have obtained that freehold land measuring 6 feet by 2¼, that is the only one obtainable by most Englishmen.

John Lavender, nailer, 24 . . . and his wife making 3½ inch spike nails . . . by their joint efforts can make 18s. a week, working fifteen hours per day . . . Rent and breeze would run to about 2s. 9d. per week. So that a good pair of workers, under specially favourable conditions, could only clear 15s. 3d. between them in a week of from 60 to 70 hours' unremitting toil.

It is good for a man to bear the yoke in his youth (how about woman?). Let them work on, good souls; parish coffins await them; skilly (a nourishing diet) awaits them in the workhouse; and, best of all, the praise of all well-meaning thick-headed men who know that labour ennobleth man, but are determined to be as little noble themselves as possible. Again:

One little shop was in full swing . . . four young women, all clean and newly washed, had just resumed nail making after tea. Three of them at nails known as "forties," that is, 40 lbs. to the 1,000. The nails are 3 inches long, and the price 2s. 1d. per bundle of 54 lbs. These young women seem very skilful workers, and the rapidity with which they can beat, point, cut off and head the nails, seems the very culmination of manual dexterity. But working from six in the morning to nine at night, they can each make a bundle in two days, or about 6s. 3d. per week. Out of that 5d. each per week for breeze, 2d. each for rent of shop, and about 4d. per week for repair of tools. The clear earnings of these young women, skilful, persistent, unwearying workers, their arms thin but hardened by unceasing toil, their chests flat, their faces pallid, and their palms and fingers case-hardened by bellows, hammer, and rod, will run to 5s. 5d. per week when in full work. Their hours of toil are supposed to be limited by Act of Parliament.

These fair young women must be indeed noble, if work can do it.

I will quote one more instance from the report, this time of a chainmaker, a desperate, wicked old rascal, as will be seen:

An old man of 68, named Blunt . . . been a chainmaker 54 years . . . is making bare 3-8 chains, for which he can get 3s. 6d. a cwt., and can make 1½ cwt. a week. In an outburst of passionate revolt against the hardness of his lot, he declares, "I often feel inclined to put myself away."

What a disgusting old man! Does he not know that to repine is unmanly and un-English? Has he not heard the clergyman preach contentment? Did he never hear of the ultimate fate of the suicide? I hate to hear of such cases. Perhaps the unthankful old dog will be getting questions asked in Parliament, and parading his insolent starvation in that august assembly, coming between us and the Irish Question. Why can he not turn his face to the wall, curse

God, and die, like many another professing but starving Christian has to do in this famed land?

> Passing from Cradley Heath to Cradley proper (says the report) I mount to Anvil Yard, a region of squalor and dirt far surpassing anything I had yet seen. Rents are high here, and range from 3s. to 4s. In one case, a covered drain running past the end of a dwelling-house struck damp through the house wall from floor to ceiling; open drains everywhere carrying off household refuse, and ruinous privies, with overflowing ashpits, loading the atmosphere with the most pungent odours. Here, also, are the little domestic workshops, built on to the houses, so that the occupant can step at once from kitchen to anvil.

All this, too, from a Government report, prepared for that smuggest and most Philistine of legislative assemblies—the British House of Commons.

However, I have seen it all—and worse. I have seen three generations of chainmakers, from the old man of 70 to the boy of 13, working in one shop. I have seen the pallid, flat-chested girls, and I have waded through the black clinging mud of Anvil Yard. I have wondered at the patience of these unfortunate people, and I have marvelled at the supineness of Parliament, which for the last fifty years has known of their condition, and done nothing.

I challenge contradiction to my statement that the average earnings in the chainmaking trade, after deducting cost of fuel, repair of tools, etc., are: of women 4s. to 5s. 6d., with many as low as 2s. 6d.; of men, many as low as 5s., the average from 10s. to 13s., while the maximum earned by a few of the most skilful at the best quality of work is 17s. to 20s. These sums are earned by an average of twelve to fifteen hours' hard work per day. These, too, are the present figures, which are the highest earned for many years.

It now remains for me to state to what I think their misery is due, and to try to propose a remedy.

Of course, primarily, the fault is in our social system that regards toil as good in itself instead of as a necessary evil, that permits free trade in human flesh, that hugs itself with complacency as it repeats the capitalistic dogma that competition is the soul of business. Of course application of machinery has rendered the living of the nailmakers more precarious. But it is not so with the chainmakers. Small chains are not made by machinery. If a dog chain made at Cradley Heath for a penny, or at most twopence, is sold in London to the dowager to lead her phlegmatic pug for 1s., surely some one must make a dishonestly large profit out of it. I do not assert that any one person has the "legitimate shent per shent" out of it, but there are a great number of small profits made as it passes through the hands of agents and dealers, most of whom are unnecessary to its distribution. Hence it will be seen that any plan that aims at helping the chainmakers must include also a scheme for eliminating the middlemen. The truck system, too, still flourishes in the district, with the usual consequences. These reasons, the want of union, the rapacity of employers, the introduction of female labour, the scandalous neglect of Parliament to act upon the evidence of the various commissions and reports it has received, are, I think, the chief causes of the misery of the district.

As for the remedies, they are not so easily to be found. Mr. Burnett, in his report, speaks of the desirability of introducing the factory system, and further on, if I understand him rightly, seems to deprecate any legislation.

To introduce the factory system without legislation would do more harm than good. The factory system under some benevolent, go-as-you-please, supply and demand, church and chapel-going capitalist, would indeed be handing over the poor people to be more sweated than ever. I can easily imagine the abolition of the domestic workshop system and the introduction of factories on the free competitive system being used still further to sweat the people, for without doubt there is still marrow in their bones for the clever man of business to extract if he had the chance. The factory system that I look for is one under the direct control of a local authority created by the Government and elected by the chain and nail makers themselves.

I can imagine that the very idea of such a scheme would be as pleasing to the ordinary middle-class Liberal or Tory, as was the mass to the lug of Jennie Geddes.[2] A Government exists, however, I suppose, for some other purpose than to waste the nation's money in armies, in ironclads (to be sold soon for scrap iron), in pensions, and in Jubilees. Surely some portion of the wealth that has been wrung out of this unlucky district might be put at its disposal in the form of a loan. Perhaps, though, their patience has had its usual reward—neglect. If there had been park railings to pull down or landlords to boycott, the result might have been different.

Why should not the Government create a local authority with power to deal with the difficulty, as suggested by Mr. Mahon, and stated in detail on page 113?[3] These men ask no charity, only the right to live by their own work. Land might be acquired, and factories built in which the hours of labour could be limited, and the employment of women and children regulated. By the application of the steam fan, the hard degrading toil of many of the boys and girls could be dispensed with. Agents could be employed to buy the iron, fuel, and other materials for the workers, and the sale and distribution as well as the production of chains managed. In this way the workers would escape the foggers, sweaters, warehousemen, middlemen—and whatever else the parasites be called.

I believe all this could be done, and done easily, too, despite the cries sure to be raised of socialism and the like. I can imagine, though, the rage of the sweaters and the capitalists when they see a chance of their victims escaping them any other way than by death.

I know the pressure that would be brought to bear upon Parliament by the employers of labour on both sides of the House. I can fancy the cries of "Utopian," of "waste of public money," of "Protection," etc.

Gracefully, too, would come these arguments from a House of Commons that is to advance £5,000,000 to buy out Irish landlords and establish smaller ones; from a House of Commons that is prepared to spend money to expatriate the Highland Crofters; from a House of Commons that is prepared to vote £300,000 for river drainage in Ireland; from a House of Commons that has already voted £1,000 to encourage the Donegal Cottage Industries. No, the fact is, there is no party capital to be made out of the Chainmakers, and therefore neither party of political mountebanks will move in the matter.

There is another plan that might be adopted, though I confess it does not so much commend itself to me. Co-operative works have already been started in the district on a small scale, but are languishing for a lack of capital. The Government might advance a sum, by way of grant or loan, to aid these societies.

I am not bigotedly attached to either of these schemes and if the Government does not like them, let them or any individual produce a better, and I am sure no one will support it more enthusiastically than myself, if it is really likely to help these people.

Something, however, must be done, and done quickly, to cure this disgrace to England, this scandal to civilisation. Something that may place the chainmaker of Cradley at least on a level with the Hottentot; that may put life and hope into the hearts of the flat-chested, pallid-faced women; that may restore life and animation to the muddy, unpaved, deserted streets of Cradley; that may bring joy to its desolate homes; that may end the misery of this, the most miserable people in all miserable England.

Notes

1. By a special correspondent of the *Sunday Chronicle*. [C. G.]

2. In 1637 Jenny Geddes of Edinburgh threw her stool at Laud's bishop as he read the Collect, exclaiming as she did so, "Fause loon, would ye say Mass at my lug?"

3. On p. 113 of *The Nail and Chainmakers*, J. L. Mahon proposed that a local Board created by Parliament should take control of the workshops.

"Bloody Niggers"

That the all-wise and omnipresent God, to whom good people address their prayers, and for whose benefit, as set forth in the sustentation of his clergy, they hoard their threepenny bits all through the week, is really but a poor, anthropomorphous animal, is day by day becoming plainer and more manifest. He (Jahveh) created all things, especially the world in which we live, and which is really the centre of the universe, in the same way as England is the centre of the planet, and as the Stock Exchange is the real centre of all England, despite the dreams of the astronomers and the economists. He set the heavens in their place, bridled the sea, disposed the tides, the phases of the moon, made summer, winter, and the seasons in their due rotation, showed us the constant resurrection of the day after the death of night, sent showers, hail, frost, snow, thunder and lightning, and the other outward manifestations of his power to serve, to scourge, or to affright us, according to his will.

Under the surface of our world he set the minerals, metals, the coal, and quicksilver, with platinum, gold, and copper, and let his diamonds and rubies, with sapphires, emeralds, and the rest, as topazes, jacinths, peridots, sardonyx, tourmalines, or chrysoberyls, take shape and colour, and slowly carbonize during the ages.

Upon the upper crust of the great planet he caused the plants to grow, the trees, bushes of every kind, from the hard, cruciform-leaved carmamel to the pink-flowering Siberian willow. Palm trees and oaks, ash, plane, and sycamore, with churchyard yew, and rowan, holly, jacaranda, greenheart and pines, larch willow, and all kinds of trees that flourish, rot, and die unknown in tropic forests, unplagued by botanists, with their pestilent Pinus Smithii or Cupressus Higginbottomiana, rustled their leaves, swayed up and down their branches, and were content, fearing no axe. Canebrakes and mangrove swamps; the immeasurable extension of the Steppes, Pampas, and Prairies, and the frozen Tundras of the north; stretches of ling and heather, with bees buzzing from flower to flower, larks soaring into heaven above them; acres of red verbena in the Pampa; lilies and irises in Africa, and the green-bluish sage brush desert of the middle prairies of America; cactus and tacuaras, with istle and maguey, flax, hemp, esparto, and the infinite variety of the compositae, all praised his name.

Again, in the Sahara, in the Kalahari desert, in the Libyan sands, and Iceland, he denied almost all vegetation, and yet his work seemed good to those his creatures— Arabs, Bosjemen, reindeer, and Arctic foxes, with camels, ostriches and eider ducks who peopled his waste spaces. He breathed his breath into the nostrils of the animals, giving them understanding, feeling, power of love and hatred, speech after their fashion, love of offspring (if logic and anatomy hold good), souls and intelligence, whether he made their bodies biped or quadruped, after his phantasy. Giraffes and tigers, with jerboas, grey soft chinchillas, elephants, armadillos and sloths, ant-eaters, marmots, antelopes, and the fast-disappearing bison of

America, gnus, springboks and hartbeest, ocelot and kangaroo, bears (grisly and cinnamon), tapirs and wapiti, he made for man to shoot, to torture, to abuse, to profit by, and to demonstrate by his conduct how inferior in his conception of how to use his life, he is to them.

All this he did and rested, being glad that he had done so much, and called a world into existence that seemed likely to be happy. But even he, having begun to work, was seized with a sort of "cacoethes operandi," and casting about to make more perfect what, in fact, needed no finishing touch, he took his dust, and, breathing on it, called up man. This done he needed rest again, and having set the sun and moon just in the right position to give light by day and night to England, he recollected that a week had passed. That is to say, he thought of time, and thinking, made and measured it, not knowing, or perhaps not caring, that it was greater than himself; for, had he chanced to think about the matter, perchance, he had never chosen to create it, and then our lives had been immeasurable, and our capacity for suffering even more infinite than at present, that is, if "infinite" admits comparison. However, time being once created and man imagined (but not yet perfected), and, therefore, life the heavy burden being opposed on him, the Lord, out of his great compassion, gave us death, the compensating boon which makes life tolerable.

But to return to man. How, when, why, wherefore, whether in derision of himself, through misconception, inadvertence, or sheer malignity, he created man, is still unknown. With the true instinct of a tyrant (or creator, for both are one), he gave us reason to a certain power, disclosed his acts up to a certain point, but left the motives wrapped in mystery. Philosophers and theologians, theosophists, positivists, clairvoyants, necromancers, cabalists, with Rosicrucians and alchemists, and all the rabble rout of wise and reverend reasoners from Thales of Miletus down to Nietzsche, have reasoned, raved, equivocated, and contradicted one another, framed their cosmogonies, arcana, written their Gospels and Korans; printed their Tarot packs, been martyred, martyred others (fire the greatest syllogist on earth), and we no wiser.

Still man exists, black, white, red, yellow, and the Pintos of the State of Vera Cruz. A rare invention, wise conception, and the quintessence of creative power rendered complete by practice, for we must think that even an all-wise, all-powerful God (like ours) improves by practice.

An animal erect upon its feet, its eyes well placed, its teeth constructed to masticate all kinds of food, its brain seemingly capable of some development, its hearing quick, endowed with soul, and with its gastric juices so contained as to digest fish, flesh, grain, fruit, and stand the inroads of all schools of cookery, was a creative masterpiece. So all was ready and the playground delivered over beautiful to man, for men to make it hideous and miserable.

Alps, Himalayas, Andes, La Plata, and Vistula, Amazon, with Mississippi, Yangtsekiang and Ganges, Volga, Rhine, Elbe and Don; Hecla and Stromboli, Pichincha, and Cotopaxi, with the Istacihuatl and Lantern of Maracaibo; seas, White and Yellow, with Oceans, Pacific and Atlantic; great inland lakes as Titicaca, Ladoga, all the creeks, inlets, gulfs and bays, the plains, the deserts, the geysers, hot springs on the Yellowstone, Pitch Lake of Trinidad, and, to be brief, the myriad wonders of the world were all awaiting newly-created man, waiting his coming forth from out the bridal chamber between the Tigris and Euphrates, like a mad bridegroom to run his frenzied course. Then came the (apparent) lapsus in the creator's scheme. That the first man in the fair garden by the Euphrates was white, I think, we take for granted. True that we have no information on the subject, but in this matter of creation we have entered, so to speak, into a tacit compact with the creator, and it behoves us to concur with him and help him when a difficulty looms.

Briefly I leave the time when man contended with the mastodon, hunted the mammoth, or was hunted in his turn by plesiosaurus or by pterodactyl. Scanty indeed are the records which survive of the Stone Age, the Bronze, or of the dwellers in the wattled wigwams on the lakes. Suffice it, that the strong preyed on the weak as they still do to-day in Happy England, and that early dwellers upon earth seem to have thought as much as we do, how to invent appliances with which to kill their fellows.

The Hebrew Scriptures and the record of crimes, of violence, and bad faith committed by the Jews on other races, need not detain us, as they resemble so entirely our own exploits amongst the "niggers" of to-day. I take it that Jahveh was little taken up with any of his creatures, except the people who inhabited the countries from which the Aryans came. Assyrians, Babylonians, Egyptians, Persians and the rest were no doubt useful and built pyramids, invented hanging gardens, erected towers, observed the stars, spoke truth (if their historians lie not), drew a good bow, and rode like centaurs or like gauchos. What did it matter when all is said and done? They were all "niggers," and whilst they fought and conquered, or were conquered, bit by bit the race which God had thought of from the first slowly developed.

Again a doubt creeps in. Was the creator omniscient in this case or did our race compel him, force his hand, containing in itself those elements of empire which he may have overlooked? 'Twere hard to say, but sometimes philosophers have whispered that the Great Power was careless, working, as he did, without the healthy stimulus of competition. I leave this speculation as more fit for thimbleriggers, for casuists, for statisticians, metaphysicians, or the idealistic merchant, than for serious men.

Somehow or other the Aryans spread through Europe, multiplied, prospered, and possessed the land. Europe was theirs, for Finns and Basques are not worth counting, being, as it were, a sort of European "niggers," destined to disappear. Little by little out of the mist of barbarism Greece emerged. Homer and Socrates with Xenophon, Euripides, Pindar and Heraclitus, Bion, Anaximander, Praxiteles, with Plato, Pericles and all the rest of the poets and thinkers, statesmen and philosophers, who in that little state carried the triumphs of the human intellect, at least as far as any who came after them, flourished and died. Material and bourgeois Rome, wolf-suckled, on its seven hills waxed and became the greatest power, conquering the world by phrases as its paltry "Civis Romanus," and by its "Pax Romana," and with the spade, and by the sheer dead weight of commonplace, filling the office in the old world that now is occupied so worthily by God's own Englishmen. Then came the waning of the Imperial City, its decay illumined but by the genius of Apuleius and Petronius Arbiter. Whether the new religion which the pipe-clayed soldier Constantine adopted out of policy, first gave the blow, or whether, as said Pliny, that the Latifundia were the ruin of all Italy, or if the effeminacy which luxury brings with it made the Roman youths resemble the undersized, hermaphroditic beings who swarm in Paris and in London, no one knows.

Popes and Republics, Lombards, French and Burgundians, with Visigoths and Huns, and the phantasmagoria of hardly to be comprehended beings who struggled in the darker ages like microbes in a piece of flesh, or like the Christian paupers in an English manufacturing town, all paved the way for the development of the race, perhaps intended, from the beginning, to rule mankind. From when King Alfred toasted his cakes and made his candles marked in rings[1] (like those weird bottles full of sand from Alum Bay) to measure time, down to the period when our present Sovereign wrote her "Diary in the Highlands" is but a moment in the history of mankind. Still, in the interval, our race has had full leisure to mature. Saxon stolidity and Celtic guile, Teutonic dullness, Norman pride, all tempered with east wind, baptised with mist, narrowed by insularity, swollen with good fortune, and rendered overbearing with much wealth, have worked together to produce the type. A bold, beef-eating, generous, narrow-minded type, kindly yet arrogant; the men fine specimens of well fed animals, red in the blood and face; the women cleanly, "upstanding" creatures, most divinely tall; both sexes slow of comprehension, but not wanting sense; great feeders, lovers of strong drinks, and given to brutal sports as were their prototypes the men of ancient Rome; dogged as bull-dogs, quick to compassion for the sufferers from the injustice of their neighbours; thinking that they themselves can do no wrong, athletic yet luxurious, impatient of all hardships yet enduring them when business shows a profit or when honour calls; moralists, if such exist, and yet, like cats, not quite averse to fish when the turn serves; clear-headed in affairs, but yet idealists and, in the main, wrong-headed in their views of life; priding themselves most chiefly on their faults, and resolute to carry all those virtues which they lack at home to other lands.

Thus, through the mist of time, the Celto-Saxon race emerged from heathendom and woad and, in the fulness of the creator's pleasure, became the tweed-clad Englishman. Much of the earth was his, and in the skies he had his mansion ready, well aired, with every appliance known to modern sanitary science waiting for him with a large bible on the chest of drawers in every room. Australia, New Zealand, Canada, India, and countless islands, useful as coaling stations and depots where to stack his bibles for diffusion amongst the heathen, all owned his sway. Races, as different from his own as is a rabbit from an elephant, were ruled by tweed-clad satraps expedited from the public schools, the universities, or were administered by the dried fruits culled from the Imperial Bar. But whilst God's favoured nation thus had run its course, the French, the Germans, Austrians, Spaniards, Dutch, Greeks, Italians, and all the futile remnant of mankind outside "our flag" had struggled to equal them. True that in most particulars they were inferior. Their beer was weak, their shoddy not so artfully diffused right through their cloth, their cottons less well "sized," the Constitution of their realm less nebulous, or the Orders of their Churches better authenticated, than were our own. No individual of their various nationalities, by a whole life of grace was ever half so moral, as the worst of us is born. And so I leave them, weltering in their attempts to copy us, and turn to those of whom I wished to write when I sat down, but the exordium, which of course I had to write, has stood so long between us that I fear my readers, if I happen to attain to such distinction, are wondering where the applicability of the title may be described.

I wished to show, as Moses told us, that God made the earth and made it round, planted his trees, his men and beasts upon it, and let it simmer slowly till his Englishman stood forth. It seemed to me his state was become almost anthropomorphous, and I doubted, if, after all, he was so wise as some folks say. In other portions of the earth as Africa, America, Australia, and in the myriad islands of the South Seas people called "niggers" live.

What is a "nigger"? Now this needs some words in order to explain his just position. Hindus, as Brahmins, Bengalis, dwellers in Bombay, the Cingalese, Sikhs and Pathans, Rajpoots, Parsis, Afghans, Kashmiris, Beluchis, Burmese, with all the dwellers from the Caspian Sea to Timur Laut, are thus described. Arabs are "niggers."

So are Malays, the Malagasy, Japanese, Chinese, Red Indians, as Sioux, Comanches, Návajos, Apaches with Zapatecas, Esquimaux, and in the south Ranqueles, Lengwas, Pampas, Pehuelches, Tobas, and Araucanos, all these are "niggers" though their hair is straight. Turks, Persians, Levantines, Egyptians, Moors, and generally all those of almost any race whose skins are darker than our own, and whose ideas of faith, of matrimony, banking, and therapeutics differ from those held by the dwellers of the meridian of Primrose Hill, cannot escape. Men of the Latin races, though not born free, can purchase freedom with a price, that is, if they conform to our ideas, are rich and wash, ride bicycles, and gamble on the Stock Exchange. If they are poor, then woe betide them, let them paint their faces white with all the ceruse which ever Venice furnished, to the black favour shall they come. A plague of pigments, blackness is in the heart, not in the face, and poverty, no matter how it washes, still is black.

In the consideration of the "nigger" races which God sent into the world for whites (and chiefly Englishmen) to rule, "niggers" of Africa occupy first place. I take it Africa was brought about in sheer ill-humour. No one can think it possible that an all wise God (had he been in his sober senses) would create a land and fill it full of people destined to be replaced by other races from across the seas. Better, by far, to have made the "niggers" white and let them by degrees all become Englishmen, than put us to the trouble of exterminating whole tribes of them, to carry out his plan. At times a thinking man knows scarcely what to think, and sometimes doubts whether he is the God we took him for and if he is a fitting Deity for us to worship, and if we had not better, once for all, get us a God of our own race and fitted for our ways. "Niggers" who have no cannons, and cannot construct a reasonable torpedo, have no rights. "Niggers" whose lot is placed outside our flag, whose lives are given over to a band of money-grubbing miscreants (chartered or not) have neither rights nor wrongs. Their land is ours, their cattle, fields, their houses, their poor utensils, arms, all that they have; their women, too, are ours to use as concubines, to beat, exchange, to barter for gunpowder or gin, or any of the circulating media that we employ with "niggers"; ours to infect with syphillis, leave with child, outrage, torment, and make by consort with the vilest of our vile, more vile than beasts. Cretans, Armenians, Cubans, Macedonians, we commiserate, subscribe, and feel for, our tender hearts are wrung when "Outlanders" cannot get votes. Bishops and Cardinals and statesmen, with philanthropists and pious ladies, all go wild about the Turks. Meetings are held and resolutions passed, articles written, lectures delivered, and the great heart of Britain stirred as if stocks were down. But "niggers," "bloody niggers," have no friends. Witness "Fraudesia,"[2] where Selous cants and Colenbrander hangs, whilst Rhodes plays "bonnet," and Lord Grey and Co. add empires to our sway, duly baptised in blood.

So many rapes and robberies, hangings and murders, blowings up in caves, pounding to jelly with our Maxim guns, such sympathy for Crete, such coyness to express opinion on our doings in Matabeleland; our clergy all dumb dogs, our politicians dazed about Armenia; "land better liked than niggers," "stern justice meted out"—can England be a vast and seething mushroom bed of base hypocrisy, and our own God, Jahveh Sabbaoth, an anthropomorphous fool?

Notes

1. Staple industry of the Isle of Wight. [C.G.]
2. "Fraudesia" was Graham's sarcastic nickname for Rhodesia.

The Real Equality of the Sexes

In the actual struggle for the franchise now going on, I am but little interested. It is certainly a great movement and a just one, but the franchise, to men, has proved but a broken reed, as far as social freedom is concerned, and there is no apparent reason why it should prove more potent in the hands of women.

My real sympathy is with their social and economic freedom. Almost every institution, economic, social, political and religious (especially religious) is designed, or has become without designing, a means to keep women dependent upon men.

Now men nowadays have a hard enough struggle to keep themselves, and it is to their manifest advantage that women should be able to maintain and fend for themselves in life.

As to the servitude that our present political system brings on women, have not a thousand eloquent feminine tongues set it forth, throughout the length and breadth of the land?

No man can add anything to what they have said, except in the peculiarly masculine realm of humour. It would appear that wit is a feminine and humour a masculine quality, and it is doubtful if even adult suffrage will ever remedy this state of things. It has, however, often struck me that a convention of the most foolish women in Great Britain, chosen with the greatest care by the most incompetent of the female electorate, could not well be foolisher than is the British House of Commons, elected as it is at present entirely by men.

That the present political system is a potent engine for the subjection of women, anyone who has ever been at an election can at once understand.

We know that Englishmen are free and equal before the law, yet no country exists where there is greater division of classes, except perhaps the United States. One man is a bounder, another a barbarian, a third a sanguinary Jew, a fourth a snuffling Nonconformist, a fifth a bigoted Catholic, a sixth a stuck-up Churchman. A soldier is said to be narrow, a tradesman mean, a politician a shuffler, a stockbroker a cheat, a lawyer a deceiver, a doctor a fee-hunter, and "to lie like a vivisector" has become a proverb. Yet, in the mass we are all "God's Englishmen," and at election time we are assured that the Lord himself being but imperfectly equipped for the task of creation, left the world unfinished for us to correct its shortcomings. But below all these divisions, and ticketed persons, there yet exists a lower abyss. The working classes, before whom we all truckle, but whom we heartily despise in our hearts, are the real objects of our scorn. You make a fool of the working-man, says the Tory to the Liberal, and then the speaker sneaks out to see what he can do to secure the vote of the Helot at the next election.

Needless to say, both Tory and Radical amongst their friends speak patronisingly but disparagingly of the class on whose backs they climb into front seats at the national hog-trough. There comes an election, and both parties drag themselves on their bellies before the class they despise, and each professes his admiration of the virtues, the sobriety, the perseverance, the uncomplainingness of the class for whose thriftlessness, unreasonableness, insolence, and incapacity they have no words hard enough to stigmatize. And so with women; all their frivolity, their love of change, their want of grasp of a political situation, and their other mental and moral failings about which we hear so much nowadays when two or three (men) are gathered together, would all be overlooked when their votes were required for some great "cause" or another. Women should not forget that a "cause" is the means whereby a politician is put into the position of being able to plunder the nation; and they should not forget that if on the whole our politicians are honest over the counter, that in the "jug and bottle" department of contracts, making use of knowledge acquired on the Stock Exchange and the like, that when the south wind blows they can tell a hawk from a hernshaw. So that the first step to political consideration is obviously the vote, though it would do little enough towards complete emancipation, which, of course, is an economic and a sexual affair, for them.

It is conceivable that every political disability now relating to women might be swept away and that wages become equal for equal quantity and quality of work done by men and women, and yet the position of women be but little really altered unless the existing social and religious institutions and the views incident to the prevalence of these institutions were radically changed.

That way alone leads to emancipation, although the franchise may do some little good, if only at election time. Woman's emancipation is first an economic and then a sexual and religious matter after all. Once alter all the laws which set up property above mere human beings and women will be free, and man also, for women agitators

always forget (just as men do) that to free one sex and
leave the other slaves is quite impossible. In the old days in
Carolina the negro and the master both were slaves. The
Christian religion has been too readily assumed to have
been the only faith which has raised women in the social
scale.

Only repeat that which is false long enough, loud
enough, and with a sanctimonious air, and people will
believe you, although they know it is a lie. In point of fact,
it has taken nineteen hundred years for women to gain the
same equality before the law as they enjoyed in the time of
Hadrian. The Romans had a married woman's property
act at least as much in woman's favour as is our own.

During those nineteen hundred years the Church
whether Greek, Roman, Anglican, or Nonconformist has
fought against all efforts to place men and women on an
equality before the law. All know the mediaeval Church's
attitude towards woman as a sex. She was unclean, a snare,
the undoer of mankind. Virginity was placed above the
maternal state, thus showing that the Church thought she
knew better what was good for us than did the power she
knew as God. Only when priests were feed and Latin
mumbled was commerce between the sexes aught but a
deadly sin.

Thus did the Church degrade both sexes, and constitute
itself the universal brothel-keeper of mankind. Its sacra-
mental marriage, which at first was but a means of reg-
ulating natural affection for the priests' benefit, become in
the lawyer's hands an instrument for the protection of
property, and women, being weaker, bore the full brunt of
any step aside when once the fees were paid and the
indecent service duly mumbled out.

Man had his children and his money protected, and his
wife became his slave, and has remained so to the present
day. She will remain so until the marriage laws are

changed; divorce (charter of liberty to women) made easy, and the dual contract made soluble at the will of both or either party to it, instead of being, as it too often is, a life-long chain. By these means, and by legitimisation of all children and the abolition of the degrading custom of making breach of promise an actionable thing, woman's true freedom will be attained.

What can be more unjust than that a man who has run his course like twenty thousand bridegrooms rolled up into one should insist on marrying what he calls "a pure girl"?

His wife should be a hardened prostitute, that is, if prostitution hardens more than does enforced celibacy. Thus, then, it seems to me, emancipation lies in ways more difficult to follow than the mere agitation for the vote. When some of these things that I have indicated have been achieved, woman will really be emancipated; and, standing on her feet, look a man squarely in the eyes and say, "I have done this or that because it was my pleasure," and the man, looking back at her, will see she is an equal, for in the freedom of the will lies true equality.

Il Gran Rifiuto

Dante refers to someone or other as having made *il gran rifiuto*—that is, the great renunciation.[1] The phrase referred, it is believed, to some Pope or other, possibly the old hermit who was raised to the papacy, and, getting sick of it, resigned. Possibly he was an Urban. No matter who he was, he has been gibbeted for all time, by Dante, as one who could not face his opportunities.

The race is not extinct.

Never has the Trades Union Congress had such a chance as had the Congress which recently finished its inglorious week at Newcastle.

Memories are short in England—so short, that almost before the blood is dry the recollection of the dead is gone. Therefore, it may be well to remind your readers that the most Liberal Government that we have ever known has, but three weeks ago, shot several citizens, and parcelled out all England, just as if it were South Africa (during the war), into some twenty military districts.[2]

There are those who think the whole affair was planned and instigated by the same brain out of whose Pia Mater came the idea of blowing up the Mahdi's tomb,[3] throwing his body into the Nile, and cutting off his head to serve, perhaps, as a mere mess-room curiosity, till even Lord Cromer was ashamed, and took it out of the barbarian's hands.

All the above is to remind your readers that Featherstone and Denshawai,[4] our extra-legal ways in India, and the reception of the blood-stained Czar, have passed, as it would seem, quite disregarded by free Englishmen. However, here was a case where Englishmen themselves had been shot down; where every principle of English jurisprudence had been set at naught, and where proceedings for which we have no precedent but that of Cromwell, have placed all England under military law.

One would have thought at such a time that there would have been some little effervesence amongst the members of the Parliament of Labour sitting at Newcastle-on-Tyne. Nothing was further from their minds.

The business, so to speak, was opened with prayer. That is to say, the Mayor received the delegates, buttered them properly, and spoke of the great advances made by Labour since the time he was a boy. The customary excursions (one regrets the absence of alarums) then took place. They duly chose the chairman, pitching, of course, upon a very, very moderate man. The stage was set. Upon the platform sat the Cabinet: almost all moderate men, except Will Thorne.

It is strange the Parliament of Labour models itself so closely on the Parliament of Privilege and Wealth. Both have their Cabinets. Practically these Cabinets entirely supersede the Parliament. That is to say, they form the laws or resolutions, depute their Ministers to give them out, and pull the strings, and thus reduce the members or the delegates to registering machines. In both the Parliaments the members deserve all that they get, for they are willing, or at least consenting, slaves. In neither Parliament is there the faintest spirit of revolt. Respectability has breathed its deadening fumes into their hearts. No one must step outside the unities; no one must make a scene. Lo, the well-known and hardy annuals all appeared again, and time was lost, as usual, in passing resolutions—some purely academical, and others designed to advertise those who contrived them.

All the hotels were packed with special correspondents. *The Swankers' Times, The Daily Liar, The Evening Sneak Thief, Janus's Gazette,* and *Diddlesex Review,* all—all the reptile press—was represented in full force. All were agog for copy. It seemed to them that this time even the Trades Union Congress would furnish forth some good material worthy to print in leaded type. They all opined that an attack, violent and outspoken, would be made upon the Government. Down to the hall they went, sharpening their pencils, as merry as a crowd going to a football match. At last, they thought, they were about to see some fun. Their bench was all electric. They sat, their heads upon one side, just like a row of parrots in a bird-fancier's shop, alert, expectant, ready to chronicle the fiery periods that they thought would blaze, like comets, from Labour's champions.

They sat, and by degrees their air of interest was dulled, and they began to read the newspapers, though why a special correspondent should read a newspaper, seeing he knows the kind of stuff he puts into it himself, passes my powers of mind. And as they sat—but now listless and inattentive—the dull debates dragged on. Ten struck, eleven, and then twelve. At half-past twelve came the expected, long-desired, frontal attack upon the Government that did not hesitate to shoot. The correspondents cocked their ears, a flutter of paper floated from their bench, just as in old-time Scottish churches one used to hear the rustle of the Bible leaves when all the congregation "fizzled" for the text, and "raxed" the peppermints. What happened everybody knows: either from the Act of God, by barratry of mariners, pirates, the King's enemies, or rats (as bills of lading say) the whole debate fell through.

On thinking the thing over, I incline to the belief that, after all, Rats were the cause that brought the ship to grief. It seems incredible otherwise that the delegates of Labour, assembled in high conclave, should practically kiss the muzzles of the guns that shot their brothers, had not Rats got into the ship.

Here was an opportunity that never had occurred before. For once the Press, that cares as much for the Trades Union Congress as I care about the continuation of the monarchy, was out on the alert. Had the Trades Union Congress only risen to the occasion, and after a debate in which speaker after speaker had denounced the Government in unmeasured terms, comparing Mr. Churchill, say, to Mezentief[5] or to the Czar, calling down vengeance on the heads of Asquith and of George,[6] and protesting against Kitchener, who, no doubt, advised and organized the Military Blood Picnic, all England would have rung.

All the elementary laws of what we call the British Constitution had been abrogated. Military, for the first time since Cromwell, had been given a free hand. The country had been placed beneath the iron heel, and yet this was the moment that the Trades Union Congress took to come and kiss the ammunition boot, all meekly on their knees. Some little protest, certainly, was made against the presence of two meek and mild officials of the Board of Trade—men so respectable, so moderate, and so quiet that you might stuff the world with them, and no one could be sure if they were living men or but the ghosts of dead, departed office-seekers. What did it matter if they sat upon the platform, or in the council of the Girls' Friendly, or Mission to the Jews? All working men who take a place under a Liberal or Tory Government are as much castrated in their minds, as those unfortunates who, in Constantinople, guard the Sultan's slaves are in their bodies. Neither need muzzles because they cannot bite. A little mumbling and all is done with either of this kind.

What seemed so strange for the few foreigners who saw the sorry scene was that no ten or twenty stood up, like Peter, and were bold. If there had been, as there were even in Sodom, ten or twelve just men, the situation would have been saved. The effect of the fifty, thirty, twenty, or but ten leaving the hall, all in a body, conducted by the police, would still have been most damaging to Churchill, Asquith, and to George.

Nothing was done; the "comrades," a journalist observed, were "nicely jockeyed once again." And when the lunch-bell rang the Great Renunciation was accomplished, and the Trades Union Congress had swallowed its own blood.

P.S.—Thorne's Citizen Army got a little in confusion at its first manoeuvres, not owing to Thorne's fault, for he spoke well and vigorously, but because he quite forgot to say who was to have the power to dispose of it.[7] Personally, I hate all armies, citizen or otherwise, and confidently look forward to the time when guns and soldiers all will be relegated to the museum, ticketed "obsolete."

Notes

1. Dante, *Inferno*, III, 59–60.
2. In the summer of 1911, the Home Secretary (Winston Churchill) had put Britain under military control in response to widespread industrial unrest. At Liverpool and Llanelly, rioters or demonstrators had been shot by troops.
3. In 1885 the Mahdi's forces had killed General Gordon; in 1898 Major (later Lord) Kitchener's forces desecrated the Mahdi's tomb.
4. During the miners' strike at Featherstone in 1893, two men had been shot and killed by troops: see Graham's tale "A Yorkshire Tragedy." In 1906, at

Denshawai (in Egypt), a British officer had died after a fracas between soldiers and villagers; subsequently four villagers were publicly hanged, eight were jailed and others were flogged.

5. I.e., Mesentsov, the Russian police chief who had been stabbed to death by Graham's campaigning acquaintance, Stepniak.

6. Herbert Asquith, Liberal Prime Minister, and David Lloyd George, Liberal Chancellor of the Exchequer.

7. Will Thorne, M.P., had seconded a proposal for the formation of a "Citizen's Army."

The Enemy

Sometimes I think the fight for liberty is harder here with us than it is elsewhere.

In Russia, for example, there exists a social liberty such as we Englishmen have no idea of, or can understand; but freedom as we know it is quite unknown in things political.

People who write of life in Moscow or St. Petersburg describe a state of things, especially in questions which only touch the individual, which the British Philistine has never contemplated, even in his dreams.

Women and men elect to live together, dissolve their union and make other ties, and no one even criticizes, thinking such matters purely personal and of no interest to the outside world. Here, as we know, such matters form the cheap and nasty talk of everyone. In fact, they have become the staple dish, and pruriently minded men and women seem always to be prowling round trying to find out filth. Such and such a book is banned because it tries to speak the truth. A play raises a shout of execration only because some situation, which the whole world is perfectly aware often arises in men's daily lives, is touched upon. That is to say, is touched on seriously, for only let the presentation of it raise a laugh and all is well—dirt is not dirt if only you laugh at it. Thus a man when he steps into a pool of liquid road-scrapings does not soil his boots provided he has the grace to laugh.

With us, except the crimes of murder and of poverty, scarcely a crime is left but sexual irregularity. That is to say, when it happens to be found out. It ruins politicians who, had they cheated on the exchange, swindled a friend, or sold a blind man a lame horse, would have found plenty to excuse them. Breaches of good faith and integrity hardly or ever ruin public men; but breaches of the marriage laws ruin absolutely, and their damnation is eternal, both in the present world and in the next.

In Russia, whilst nothing of the above has any bearing on the public life of any man, all the world knows the state of tyranny under the Government of the Czar. One thing is certain: that in Russia the fight is not obscured as it is here with us. Tyranny and cruelty come out into the open, and all who face them do so at the peril of their lives. This makes the Russian Radical or Socialist an enemy not only both of Church and State, but of religion as it is taught, and consequently of the morality that religion inculcates. No English Radical that I have ever met comprehends this attitude, and too few Socialists. You cannot both serve God and Mammon, say the Scriptures, or, as the proverb hath it, honour and profit cannot go into the same bag.

Enemies of the present state of things must be enemies not only of the State and all its works, political and economical, but of the Churches and their moralities and faiths.

There is no other halting-place for Socialists: either they must reject the whole, or swallow all—or not be honest.

How miserable it is to see a man who calls himself a rebel run to a church to save his soul. First let him satisfy himself he really has a soul to save, and then if he is anxious on the matter let him save it by good works.

Nothing is more immoral (as I see things) than what the

ordinary Liberal calls morality. To bring morality back to its real meaning, or, if you like it better, to evolve a new and reasonable morality, that is the problem for us all. Which of us has not heard a small-souled man, a crafty bargainer, hard to the weak and cringing to the strong, described as a good man, only because no woman ever tempted him? Yet to call such a creature virtuous is to misuse the word, to tamper with first principles, and erects a vicious standard by means of which all the most vicious attributes of man are overlooked. Such men swarm thick as flies amongst the Liberals, and the fact that such false standards are accepted, often by Socialists themselves, renders the fight for Liberty as hard, or harder, with ourselves as it is in any country in the world.

When once Goliath stalks into the field, no matter how huge be his shield, how vast his strength, or what the weight and sharpness of his lance, David can match him with his sling. In England, the giant has the cunning of the serpent, in addition to his strength. David, with us, may smite him all over with his smoothest pebbles from the brook, not that he slings over-much, though, for English David is a prudent youth; but none of all his missiles find their mark. The fact is, there is no particular mark to aim at. The armour is so cunningly contrived that it is quite invisible; but at the same time, equally impenetrable to attack. The sweater cries out, "Hit the landlord. St. Smug for Liberalism!" The landlord yells, "Down with the sweater!" Both of them cry, "St. George for Merry England!" Thus the Reformer, Socialist, Radical, Anarchist, or what not, stands like a bull in the arena, pawing the sand and bellowing with fury, but impotent to strike. The attempt to hold at one and the same time Socialist views of economics, and Christo-bourgeois views of what the bourgeois Liberal calls "morality," is the chief difficulty that the reformer finds athwart his path.

Each system of society must have a system of morality

suitable to its needs. The remains of feudalism that till a short ten years ago lingered in rural England, were like germs of a disease. So with the system of morality that holds a sexual offence more serious than the most miserable crime against mankind.

No thinking man or woman preaches universal licence. Not that they think that it would be a crime against religion, still less because they think such matters have any real concern with what is called society; but they all know that were it general it would be a crime against the race. Drunkenness, gluttony, cruelty to children and to animals, cheating and sweating, suppression of the truth and defamation, all are far worse offences against mankind than is the overstepping of the line of conduct that Liberal politicians call "the moral code." Let us see, now, how it works out. In my own recollection I have known three or four public men, men honourable and true, reformers, honest in money matters, and above reproach in all their dealings with their fellow-men in most respects, struck down and howled at for errors in a matter which their accusers were exempt from, perhaps from lack of opportunity, or of iron in the blood. No doubt they would have said (patting their paunches): "Our lives at least are clean!" Strange that the men who heard them should not have perceived that usurers, oppressors of their fellows, gluttons, and money-grubbers do not live pure lives. The reason no one saw the fallacy of what they said was because so many advanced thinkers on economics, sociology, and the like are still slaves to the ethics of a bygone age.

This comes from Puritanism, and Puritanism in its very essence is rank tyranny. Moreover, a mean, spying, prurient-minded tyranny. They say that many multi-millionaires, those who endow towns with a public lavatory (but without funds to keep it up), that oil and iron lords, compared to whom our richest dukes are just as poor as is our Chancellor, are churchgoers, deeply religious and the husbands of one wife. What if it is so? Those private virtues have nothing in the world to do with public life. As well when a man sings out of tune and people hiss, exclaim: "He is a Wesleyan!" as to bring forth the private virtues of a sweater as an excuse for him if he shoots down his workmen at a strike.

This strange inversion of the importance of public and of private actions, derived from Puritanism, and still prevailing in the United States, where men call actions "smart" that would make devils grin, is, above all things, the chief reason for the low ideals of all public life. Get rich, by all means that you can, only get rich, and all the rest will be forgiven to you. That is our practice, no matter what the motto that we use. Be pure in private; but in public intrigue, suppress the truth, condone oppression of the weak (as at Denshawai, Casablanca, or in Tripoli), break every pledge, attribute every low-souled motive to opponents, bully small nationalities, blow wretched negro huts to pieces with shells of melinite, cringe to the knout-Czar: it is all right so that you never have fallen into the only sin that damns a Liberal plutocrat—that is to say, if he is caught, and has not time to pay. As well attempt to console a man whose wife has run off with a friend, by saying that the seducer in his capacity as secretary to his local golf club was an honourable man, and in the House of Commons voted Liberal.

I see the enemy in what is called the Cocoa Press,[1] just as a Frenchman or a Spaniard sees him in the Church. We all distrust those who put on an air of being better than mankind. If angels were volplaned suddenly to earth, the chances are that we should loathe them for their superior virtue. How much more shall we loathe those who see all there is to see in modern life—its littleness, its infinite meanness, lack of all ideal, its cruelty, oppression of the weak, its gloom and ugliness—and, standing in their pulpits, bless their Lord that it is good, fair, honourable, improving every day, and that all wrongs will shortly be redressed.

The enemy is he who knows all this but seeks to stop others knowing it; the man who, always anxious to spy out the private faults of private men, condones the public shortcomings of those of his own party, when the first should be looked at with charity as perhaps incidental to our nature, the others scourged with chains.

Note

1. An example of the "Cocoa Press" was the Liberal *Daily News,* owned by a Quaker, George Cadbury, the wealthy head of a cocoa and chocolate firm.

Scotland's Day: 21st June, 1930

Mr. Chairman, ladies and gentlemen, we stand once more on this historic ground. The surroundings are unaltered. The eternal hills still form our background. Stirling Castle, a perennial monument to the power of Scotland when she shook the might of England to the core, makes our middle distance. Not far from where we are to unfold this banner is the historic Borestone whence the banner of the Bruce fluttered on the greatest occasion whereon victory has crowned the arms of Scotland. Three miles from here Wallace broke Cressingham upon the long bridge over the Forth. Where'er I look, north, south, east or west, there is something that appeals to me as a Scotsman, there is something to stir one's heart, something to make one feel that we are representatives of a distinct nationality—a nationality severed from all other nationalities and as different from our friends in England as we are from the Germans, the French, the Russians, or any other nationality. The British Empire today has become a confederation of varying States. Australia, New Zealand, British Columbia, the Cape Colonies, and all the rest of the dependencies have got their Parliaments and their separate legislatures.

They are all practically self-governing States within their boundaries, and I ask you, is Scotland inferior to any one of these nationalities? Did we not send out the best and bravest of our sons to colonise Canada, New Zealand, Australia, and wherever the flag of the British Empire flies? I ask you as Scottish men and women whether it is not an injustice that cries out to heaven and a sin against political science that the one nationality—the oldest of those that I have mentioned, and older perhaps than England itself, as a separate State—should be subservient to them, a mere appendage to the predominant partner, a mere county of England, such as Yorkshire, Lancashire, Nottingham or Middlesex. I, for one, cannot sit calmly under such a supposition.

They tell us—triflers, pifflers and writers in the Press—that we rule the British Empire. That is untrue. What is true is that individual Scotsmen hold high posts in the British Empire. Why do they hold them? They hold them because of their abilities, not because of their nationality as Scotsmen. If a man applies for any situation they do not ask him first, Are you a Catholic, a Protestant, a Presbyterian, a Czecho-Slovak, an American, an Englishman or a Scotsman, but they take the best man for their purpose, and that is why individual Scotsmen hold high positions in the Empire. To say that we rule the Empire is an untruth, and those who state it know it is an untruth.

Let us assume for a moment that we did rule the Empire. What we do not rule is our own country, and I do not consider that even were the ruling of the Empire a fact instead of a myth, that it would in any wise repay us for the position of inferiority into which we have been relegated, perhaps not by the fault of Englishmen, but by our own apathy, and by our own dislike to go forward and face the petty martyrdom that we should have to endure.

Nationality is in the atmosphere of the world. Within the last ten years we have seen twenty nationalities come into being—Czecho-Slovakia, Yugo-Slavia, Poland, Lithuania, Esthonia, Ireland, and perhaps there are others in the making even today. Shall Scotland lag behind all these nationalities? We talk about our prayer for a good conceit of ourselves. I used to think it was a prayer that was scarcely worth being put up by Scotsmen, but today it is a prayer that every Scottish man and woman should keep in mind, and should perpetually put up until we have achieved what we have in view, complete autonomy for our native land.

When James VI was a little boy they took him to the old Parliament House in Stirling, and looking up he saw there was a tile or two off the roof, and he said "There is ane hole in this Parliament." The Parliament House still stands. As to the condition of its roof I know but little, but as for the condition of its interior I am well aware. No Scottish Parliament, no single representative of Scotland sits with plenary power to legislate for his own land, either in the old Parliament House of Stirling or in Edinburgh, and it is a disgrace to all Scotsmen that they do not sit there. I lay upon you as a sacred duty that you agitate until our old Parliament is restored to us, and once again Scotland takes her place as an independent nationality in the family of nations.

Let us for a moment survey what has been going on in the English Parliament. We have seen practically the bankruptcy of all political parties. Mr. Baldwin and his happy family are struggling for leadership and for autonomy in their party. Mr. Lloyd George continues to twankle the Welsh harp and to deal out the dollars to those who have received his imprimatur. And the Labour Party is almost like a hornet's nest, each member of it, with true Christian unction, doing as much as possible to tread upon the hands of those who are slowly mounting the ladder. But let us be just, there is one thing the Labour Party have done for us. They have given us an increased income tax, and Mr. Lansbury has instituted mixed bathing in the Serpentine. That is about the achievement at the present except the daily culture of the unemployed, who are growing like Jonah's gourd while they are sleeping. That is about the *summum bonum* of the achievement of the Governmental party at present in power.

In times gone by with old Keir Hardie and others, I was one of those who fought for the establishment of a Labour Party. I was young in those days and I had my illusions thick upon me. I hoped the coming of the Labour Party would be the coming of the millennium in England and Scotland. I was disappointed. They have simply become a party struggling for office and place like any of the other parties, and although every one of them are lavish of promises when they are out of office, I see no responsible statesman or highly placed member of one of the three parties who has devoted a speech or motion in the House of Commons—or introduced any legislation—dealing exclusively with Scotland. Therefore I conclude that it is vain for Scotsmen to look for help in their struggle for autonomy to any of the existent parties.

People have said that we shall lose by Scottish autonomy. They would have us imagine that we were mere barbarians before the Union. Some gentlemen the other day painted an awful picture of Scotland before England took it by the hand. We believed in witchcraft, our feudal barons oppressed their people, the miners were practically serfs, and culture was unknown throughout the land. At that very time what was the state of England? Was England a paradise? Did the proletariat of England have any votes? Were not the feudal land-owners of England to the full as arrogant and as ignorant of the conditions of their fellow men as the feudal land-owners of Scotland?

It is a pretence and a sham that Scotland owes its prosperity to the Union with England. Did England gain nothing by the Union? Were the benefits upon one side? Was it no small benefit for any country to receive a population of hardy, industrious, brave and valiant men within her bounds, from which she could, and did, recruit her armies, putting the Scottish regiments always in the forefront of the battle? Had I lived in the time of the Union with England I would have resisted it to the best of my ability with Fletcher of Saltoun, and had it gone to arms I would have been beside the Scottish patriots. The prosperity of Scotland was induced by the economic progress of the world. It was not in England's power even if she had wished to do so, to withhold the benefits that naturally accrued by the increasing wealth of Europe from Scotland. Scotland merely shared in the same development that touched France, Germany, Italy, Spain and the United States; and those who wish to take us back to these times, and paint a derogatory portrait, are no true Scotsmen, and what is left for them is to bow before the golden calf of England, and to kiss the rod that chastises them.

There are many ways in which we can achieve self-government for Scotland. We are not called upon to martyr ourselves and endure persecution, death or imprisonment, as were the Irish. It is a very simple process. We have merely to vote and to signify our wishes to the Parliament of Great Britain, and Scottish Home Rule would be as certain as that day follows night. I have been asked what should be the first movement of Scottish Nationalists were they returned to the British Parliament with a majority and a mandate, if the British House of Commons were against them. My answer has always been that they should withdraw to Edinburgh and start a Parliament which would be the beginning of our great and National Parliament. There is nothing very heroic in that. There is no great self-sacrifice. In fact it is so easy and so manifest to the poorest intelligence that I need not elaborate the point.

We want a renaissance, a re-birth of Scottish literature, art and sentiment. We can induce these things only by agitating for national self-government. Look at Southern Ireland. I do not hold it up as an example of all that mankind can achieve. I believe it is a very dull place since you do not hear the revolvers popping, but since she got self-government there has been a most marvellous renaissance of national sentiment and art, as displayed in drama, poetry and novel writing. Irish painters and poets are deriving inspiration from the old legend of their country, and from the actual conditions of their modern life. That is what I want to see in Scotland.

I cannot bear to see Scottish writers take their inspiration from English themes. I cannot bear to see our painters paint entirely English subjects. Have they no themes in Scotland; are there no tragedies in the slums of Glasgow, in the mining districts of Lanarkshire and in the Western Islands for men to write about; have our hills and straths lost their enchantment for painters? I say 'No'; but I do say that we want an increase of national sentiment in order to direct the attention of our artists and painters and poets more exclusively to the consideration of national subjects. No great movement has ever been carried to its end without idealism. A mere appeal to material improvement has never moved any mass of men; Scotsmen especially, under their somewhat hard exterior, are especially amenable to an appeal to sentiment. When Bruce unfurled his banner did he harangue his soldiers upon yonder stricken field saying that they would make more money if they conquered England? Did he hold out to them increase of wealth or of position? No, if the Archdeacon of Aberdeen, Barbour, is to be believed, he spoke to them of Liberty, an intangible thing, a mere idea.

Did William Tell make his appeal to pure materialism? Let us come to the three great Mahatmas of modern life, Gandhi, Lenin and Mussolini. You may think, two of them may not appeal to sentiment, but Lenin and Mussolini were men inbued with sentiment, and Mussolini alone with his good and his bad qualities and rule in Italy has been able to do what he has done by the appeal to Italian national sentiment.[1] I hold no brief for Mussolini; but he found Italy, the Cinderella of Europe, almost in the dust, a prey to the worst kind of anarchy—an anarchy in which the anarchist had no ideal of freedom or liberty or any competent state. He held before them the emblem of the ancient Roman Empire, and by that he has appealed to them, by that he has elevated them, and has been able to make a united country, and to carry it to the position in which we see it today. Do you suppose the men he spoke to were urged by hope of individual gain? Do you think that Gandhi, when he started his salt-making agitation imagined he was going to gain anything by it in a material sense? The salt the British Government made was no doubt one hundred times better than the salt that his Satyagrahis[2] made upon the edge of the ocean. What he appealed to was the national sentiment of Indians, and by that he was enabled to inaugurate a movement that, good or bad, has shaken the British Empire to its very core.

We must have Scottish sentiment, we must have that which elevates mankind and makes mankind superior to the inferior animals, that which unites us intimately to every object that is loved and dear to us in our own country. We must have a sentiment that shows us that the slums of Glasgow are a slur not only upon the world, but upon each and every individual one of us, that shows us that the Highlands of Scotland are not only a crying scandal to Scotland and to the Empire, but that they call aloud to us as a scandal against humanity. Think of these regions once the abode of men, poor, violent and perhaps uneducated, but still human beings, think of them today—mere playgrounds of rich men, with these mountains and straths debarred and cut off from the use of the population of the country. Think of the roads closed, the cottages pulled down, and the desolate straths that once resounded with the laughter of children and the pibroch of the piper—silent but for the clacking of the grouse, the whirring of the black cock's wings and the grunting call of the deer. I say that it is wrong and must be altered, and it lies on us as Scottish men and women to alter it, and I call upon you all here under this flag which is to be unfurled, never to cease agitating until we get that autonomy for Scotland which alone can revive our ancient spirit, and make real Scotsmen of us.

Notes

1. Graham subsequently criticized Mussolini's bombing of Abyssinia (*Mirages*, p. xii); and he had previously said that he would be delighted to recognise Lenin "at the end of a long piece of hard rope" (Watts and Davies, *Cunninghame Graham*, p. 244).

2. Gandhi advocated *Satyagraha*—the principle of passive resistance and civil disobedience.

Part III
Literary Pieces

Introduction

Cunninghame Graham's writings often treat casually the conventional generic classifications that make life easy for both the general reader and the academic critic. With a piece that is obviously a short story, patently a philosophical essay, or manifestly an autobiographical reminiscence, the critic knows where he is; but Graham feels free to roam across boundaries, treating conventional limits with the contempt that they perhaps do deserve. What at first may seem a lack of discipline in his work may yield new kinds of pleasure: partly the pleasure of the unpredictable, partly the pleasure of recognising the logic within his apparent want of method. By accident or design his writing frequently lays false trails, lulling our expectations yet finally surprising us by a close-up, an unexpected concentration on some vivid detail that casts a restrospective and transforming light on the whole. Even when there are good grounds for suspecting that he has been led astray by the *ignis fatuus* of a digression, he can still offer unpredictable rewards. A nostalgic melancholy that threatened to terminate in sentimentality may proceed to a cynical aphorism; a moralistic diatribe may conclude with a self-mocking flourish.

The following items are arranged in chronological order according to the date of the original publication; though as many of them were first printed in periodicals, the order may not be that in which they eventually appeared in book form in the various collections. The opening piece, "The Impenitent Thief," illustrates the difficulty of categorising Graham's work. It was originally published in Hyndman's *The Social-Democrat* in January 1898, in the company of predictably militant articles advocating class warfare to liberate the masses from capitalism. Yet into this belligerent company Graham introduces a meditation on St. Luke's impenitent thief, the fellow who may have been called Dimas or Gestas and who, crucified with a second malefactor alongside Jesus Christ, dared to say "If thou be Christ, save thyself and us." The essay has, certainly, its political points to make: by attacking the Christian doctrine of penitence Graham is exhorting men to stand boldly and consistently on their own feet, and possibly he has in mind the scandal caused when his acquaintance Parnell defied Victorian morality. His central point, however, is one which transcends local political concerns. Graham emphasises the common humanity which must have linked the pious malefactor with the impious one so long condemned by the Church; the essay (later included in *Success*, 1902) is therefore a fine illustration of Graham's preoccupation with the plight of underdogs past and present.

The second piece, "The Gold Fish" (*Saturday Review*, 18 February 1899; *Thirteen Stories*, 1900), is an exotic tale, leisurely in exposition. The runner's journey across the Sahara gives Graham ample opportunity to display his own first-hand knowledge of the region; and indeed he had encountered a messenger there who bore just such an improbable gift of goldfish. The ending is reminiscent of the techniques of Conrad—not surprisingly, in view of the frequency with which Graham and the Polish writer were enthusiastically exchanging publications and comparing notes at this time. What particularly brings Conrad to mind is Graham's final combination of resonantly pessimistic generalization and ruthlessly-observed grim detail, and, in addition, the sense of life's absurdities, summed up in the memorable image of the goldfish bowl gleaming bright and hard in the desert sands while its bearer lies with blackened tongue.

"A Hegira" (*Saturday Review*, 5 August 1899; *Thirteen Stories*) also lays final emphasis on a wasteful death. The tale is characteristically autobiographical: it was on a Mexican journey in 1880 that Graham's path had crossed the trail of the escaping Mescalero Indians. Again he sides with the underdog: in this case, with the Mescaleros, who seek only their homelands, but are pursued and killed, one by one, by the whites. That the cowboy is presented as a callous barbarian is typical of Graham's ability to see beyond the prejudices of his times. Not until seventy years later were the rights of the dispossessed Indians to become a familiar political topic.

Though Graham's sense of the ephemerality of life sometimes led him to sentimentality, he endeavoured constantly to criticize the gross sentimentalities of his age, and he was shrewd in noting how often they went hand in hand with callousness of one kind or another. Since its extinction, the Victorian music-hall has repeatedly been sentimentalized by commentators who regard it as splendidly full-blooded entertainment, the truly popular theatre. Graham, who had attended music-hall performances often enough, knew better. "The Pyramid" (*Justice*, 1 May 1900; *Success*, 1902) observes the prostitutes who gathered there, the vulgar patriotism of the crowds, and the hope of disaster that lurks in those who watch tricky and dangerous acrobatic acts. Graham liked to observe life from an unfamiliar and surprising angle, and here, from the wings, he sees the glint of hatred and contempt as the performers look out at the patrons beyond the footlights.

"A Yorkshire Tragedy" (in *Progress,* 1905) refers to the aftermath of the Featherstone killings of 1893. The nation's mine-owners had attempted to reduce coal-miners' wages by 25 per cent; the miners went on strike, and riots occurred at many pits which employed non-union labour. At Ackton Hall colliery, Featherstone, buildings were set ablaze by the angry crowds; the troops then made a bayonet charge and opened fire, killing James Gibbs and John Duggan. Graham had visited the scene during the disturbances, and his later speeches alluded to the event as an instance of the ruthlessness of the powers of the state in a supposedly democratic land. However, instead of the indignation of that political oratory, the article has an almost elegiac tone: the indignation is muted and reticent, and is perhaps the more effective for that restraint. The piece is somewhat Lawrentian in its depiction of blighted lives and blighted landscape.

"Beattock for Moffat," which had been published in *Success,* soon became one of the most highly rated of Graham's tales: it subsequently re-appeared in several collections and anthologies. Once regarded as poignantly realistic in its concentration on three representatives of commonplace inglorious humankind, it may now seem patronising or condescending in its scrutiny of those travellers on a fatal journey. I leave the reader to judge.

The seventh piece is an ironic requiem for the Victorian age, prompted by the national mourning for Queen Victoria herself. "Might, Majesty and Dominion" (*Saturday Review,* 9 February 1901; *Success*) shows Graham's ability to make the reader uncertain of the possible eventual outcome of the reflections before dispelling those doubts with a telling visual close-up. A more direct comment on Victoria is made in "An Idealist" (*Saturday Review,* 25 August

1906; *Faith,* 1909) by Betterton, whose pamphlet *Messalina* denounces the "brutal and licentious old queen" for the orgies of her career. Composed deliberately as a reply to Conrad's tale "An Anarchist," "An Idealist" draws on Graham's memories of an eccentric whose real name, as John Galsworthy noted, was Chatterton.

It was Galsworthy, too, who raised the question of Graham's indebtedness to Maupassant in various tales. One obvious connection is between Maupassant's "Le Port" and Graham's "Christie Christison" (*Charity,* 1912). In both, a sailor, itching with lust after months at sea, visits a brothel; and in both, the prostitute he chooses proves to be a relative: in one case, his sister; in the other, his estranged wife. Graham admired Maupassant and had long studied his works, so there may indeed be a literary debt; but this comparison indicates his superiority to the Frenchman. Maupassant expects his reader to be shocked: the seaman's extravagant horror at his unintentional incest seems to be endorsed by the narrator's stern reference to "*la couche criminelle.*" Graham's tale, on the other hand, is virtually about the merits of unshockability: it invites the reader to accept as normal and even admirable the matter-of-fact reconciliation of the couple. "Le Port" is an economical, poised narrative; "Christie Christison" uses the oblique narrative form, the tale within the tale—it is both character-study and reminiscential anecdote, freer and apparently more vagrant in structure. But the two incidents in Christie's recollections—the brothel-encounter and the meeting with an Indian who tries to buy Christie's wife from him—prove to be closely linked by an understated irony. "Christians don't sell their wives," the Indian is told; but the difference between European and Indian diminishes when the tale offers its reminder that at brothels wives are bought and sold by "Christians." The very title of the piece introduces this religious paradox.

In Graham's later writings, the ironies become less

acidic, the writing smoother, sometimes blander. Understandably, in view of his age, he becomes increasingly preoccupied by elegiac reflections. But he never lost his interest in the incongruous, the absurd, and the apparently futile life; in the obscure, vagrant figure who may die without a memorial and possibly even without identification. Death in the wilderness is seen as an acute instance of human isolation and ephemerality generally. "Animula Vagula" (*English Review*, September 1917; *Redeemed*, 1927) is a memorable example of this interest; and the desire to memorialize the fleeting encounters and vivid moments of a vanished past is the motive of "The Stationmaster's Horse" (*Library Review*, Winter 1932; *Writ in Sand*, 1932). Here Graham, writing in his eightieth year, looks back on an incident that had occurred in Paraguay more than half a century previously. As a tale, it is slight; as an *envoi* from an adventurous, vain yet engaging personality, it can be regarded as the concluding chapter in the huge work formed by all his tales and essays: an idiosyncratic and humane autobiography.

The Impenitent Thief

Dimas or Gestas, Gestas or Dimas, who can say which, when even monkish legends disagree?

At any rate, one of the two died game.

Passion o' me, I hate your penitents.

Live out your life: drink, women, dice, murder, adultery, meanness, oppression, snobbery (by which sin the English fall); be lavish of others' money, and get thereby a name for generosity. Bow down to wealth alone, discerning talent, beauty, humour (the most pathetic of all qualities), wit, courage, and pathos, only in gilded fools.

Keep on whilst still digestion waits on appetite, and at the first advance of age, at the first tinge of gout, sciatica, at the first wrinkle, crow's-foot, when the hair grows thin upon the temples, the knees get "shauchle," when the fresh horse seems wild, the jolting of the express crossing the facing points makes you contract your muscles, and when all life seems to grow flat, stale, and unprofitable outside the library, forsake your former naughty life, and straight turn traitor on your friends, ideas, beliefs, and prejudices, and stand confessed apostate to yourself. For the mere bettering of your spiritual fortunes leaves you a turncoat still. It is mean, unreasonable, and shows a caitiff spirit, or impaired intellect in the poor penitent who, to save his paltry soul, denies his life.

Dimas or Gestas, whiche'er it was, no doubt some unambitious oriental thief, a misappropriator of some poor bag of almonds, sack of grain, bundle of canes, some frail of fruit, camel's hair picket rope, or other too well considered trifle, the theft of which the economic state of Eastern lands makes capital, had given him brevet rank amongst the world's most honoured criminals, set up on high to testify that human nature, even beside a coward and a God, is still supreme.

Perhaps again some sordid knave, whipped from the markets, an eye put out, finger lopped off, nose slit, ears cropped, and hoisted up to starve upon his cross as an example of the folly of the law, crassness of reason, to appease the terrors of the rich, or, perhaps, but to exemplify that Rome had a far-reaching arm, thick head, and owned a conscience like to that enjoyed by Rome's successor in the empire of the world.

Dimas or Gestas, perhaps some cattle thief from the Hauran, some tribesman sent for judgment to Jerusalem, black bearded, olive in colour, his limbs cast like an Arab's, or a Kioway's twisted in agony, his whole frame racked with pain, his brain confused, but yet feeling, somehow, in some vague way, that he, too, suffered for humanity to the full as much as did his great companion, who to him, of course, was but a Jewish Thaumaturgist, as his adjuration, "If thou be the Son of God, save us and thyself," so plainly shows.

And still, perhaps, impenitent Gestas (or Dimas) was the most human of the three, a thief, and not ashamed of having exercised his trade. How much more dignified than some cold-hearted scoundrel who, as solicitor, banker, or confidential agent, swindles for years, and in the dock recants, and calls upon his God to pardon him, either because he is a cur at heart, or else because he knows the public always feels tenderly towards a cheat, having, perhaps, a fellow-feeling, and being therefore kind.

I like the story of the Indian who, finding his birch canoe caught in the current, and drifted hopelessly towards Niagara, ceased all his paddling when he found his efforts vain, lighted his pipe, and went it, on a lone hand, peacefully smoking, as the spectators watched him through their opera glasses.

And so perhaps this stony-hearted knave, whom foolish painters bereft of all imagination, have delighted to revile in paint, making him villainous in face, humpbacked, blind of one eye, and all of them drawing the wretched man with devils waiting for his poor pain-racked soul, as if the cross was not a hell enough for any act of man, may have repented (of his poor unsuccessful villainies) long years ago. He may have found no opportunity, and being caught red-handed and condemned to death, made up his mind to cease his useless paddling, and die after the fashion he had lived. This may have been, and yet, perhaps again, this tribesman, as the night stole on the flowers, the waters, and the stones, all sleeping, reckoned up his life, saw nothing to repent of, and thought the cross but one injustice more. As gradually hope left his weakening body, he may have thought upon the folded sheep, the oxen in their stalls, the camels resting on their hardened knees, men sleeping wrapped up in their *haiks* beneath the trees, or at the foot of walls, mere mummies rolled in white rags, under the moonbeams and the keen rays of El Sohail.[1] No one awake except himself and the two figures on his either hand, during the intolerable agony of the long hours, when jackals howl, hyenas grunt, and as from Golgotha, Jerusalem looked like a city of the dead, all hushed except the rustling of the palm trees in the breeze. Then may his thoughts have wandered to his *duar* on the plains, and in his tent he may have seen his wives, and heard them moan, heard his horse straining on his picket rope and stamping, and wept, but silently, so that his fellow sufferers should not see his tears.

And so the night wore on, till the tenth hour, and what amazed him most was the continual plaint of Dimas (or of Gestas) and his appeals for mercy, so that at last, filled with contempt and sick with pain, he turned and cursed him in his rage.

Repentance, retrospection, and remorse, the furies which beset mankind, making them sure of nothing; conscious of actions, feeling they are eternal, and that no miracle can wipe them out. They know they forge and carry their own hell about with them, too weak to sin and fear not, and too irrational not to think a minute of repentance can blot out the actions of a life.

Remorse, and retrospection, and regret; what need to conjure up a devil or to invent a place of torment, when these three were ready to our souls. Born in the weakness (or the goodness) of ourselves, never to leave us all our lives; bone of our bone and fibre of our hearts; man's own invention; nature's revenge for all the outrages we heap upon her; reason's despair, and sweet religion's eagerest advocates; what greater evils have we in the whole pack with which we live, than these three devils, called repentance, retrospection, and regret?

But still the penitent upon the other side was human too. Most likely not less wicked in his futile villainy than his brother, whom history has gone out to vilify and to hold up as execrable, because he could not recognise a god in him he saw, even as he himself, in pain, in tears, and as it seemed least fit to bear his suffering, of the three. Repentance is a sort of fire insurance, hedging on what you will—an endeavour to be all things to all men and to all gods.

Humanity repentant shows itself *en déshabillé,* with the smug mask of virtue clear stripped off, the vizor of consistency drawn up, and the whole entity in its most favourite Janus attitude, looking both ways at once. The penitent on the right hand, whom painters have set forth, a fair young man, with curly golden hair, well rounded limbs, tears of contrition streaming from his eyes, with angels hovering around his head to carry off his soul, whom writers have held up for generations as a bright instance of redeeming faith duly rewarded at the last, was to the outward faithless eye much as his brother thief.

Perhaps he was some camel driver, who, entrusted with a bag of gold, took it, and came into Jerusalem showing some self-inflicted wounds, and called upon Jehovah or Allah to witness that he had received them guarding the money against thieves. That which he said upon the cross he may have thought was true, and yet men not infrequently die, as they have lived, with lies upon their lips. He may have seen that in his fellow sufferer which compelled respect, or yet again he may have, in his agony, defied the Jews by testifying that the hated one was king. All things are possible to him who has no faith.

So, when the night grew misty towards dawn, and the white eastern mist crept up, shrouding the sufferers and blotting out their forms, the Roman soldiers keeping watch, had they looked up, could not have said which of the thieves was Gestas and which Dimas, had they not known the side on which their crosses stood.

Note

1. Canopus.

The Gold Fish

Outside the little straw-thatched café in a small court-yard trellised with vines, before a miniature table painted in red and blue, and upon which stood a dome-shaped pewter teapot and a painted glass half filled with mint, sat Amarabat, resting and smoking hemp. He was of those whom Allah in his mercy (or because man in the Blad-Allah has made no railways) has ordained to run. Set upon the road, his shoes pulled up, his waistband tightened, in his hand a staff, a palm-leaf wallet at his back, and in it bread, some hemp, a match or two (known to him as *el spiritus*), and a letter to take anywhere, crossing the plains, fording the streams, struggling along the mountain-paths, sleeping but fitfully, a burning rope steeped in saltpetre fastened to his foot, he trotted day and night—untiring as a camel, faithful as a dog. In Rabat as he sat dozing, watching the greenish smoke curl upwards from his hemp pipe, word came to him from the Khalifa of the town. So Amarabat rose, paid for his tea with half a handful of defaced and greasy copper coins, and took his way towards the white palace with the crenelated walls, which on the cliff, hanging above the roaring tide-rip, just inside the bar

106

of the great river, looks at Salee. Around the horseshoe archway of the gate stood soldiers, wild, fierce-eyed, armed to the teeth, descendants, most of them, of the famed warriors whom Sultan Muley Ismail (may God have pardoned him!) bred for his service, after the fashion of the Carlylean hero Frederick; and Amarabat walked through them, not aggressively, but with the staring eyes of a confirmed hemp-smoker, with the long stride of one who knows that he is born to run, and the assurance of a man who waits upon his lord. Some time he waited whilst the Khalifa dispensed what he thought justice, chaffered with Jewish pedlars for cheap European goods, gossiped with friends, looked at the antics of a dwarf, or priced a Georgian or Circassian girl brought with more care than glass by some rich merchant from the East. At last Amarabat stood in the presence, and the Khalifa, sitting upon a pile of cushions playing with a Waterbury watch, a pistol and a Koran by his side, addressed him thus:

"Amarabat, son of Bjorma, my purpose is to send thee to Tafilet, where our liege lord the Sultan lies with his camp. Look upon this glass bowl made by the Kaffir, but clear as is the crystal of the rock; see how the light falls on the water, and the shifting colours that it makes, as when the Bride of Rain stands in the heavens, after a shower in spring. Inside are seven gold fish, each scale as bright as letters in an Indian book. The Christian from whom I bought them said originally they came from the Far East where the Djin-descended Jawi live, the little yellow people of the faith. That may be, but such as they are, they are a gift for kings. Therefore, take thou the bowl. Take it with care, and bear it as it were thy life. Stay not, but in an hour start from the town. Delay not on the road, be careful of the fish, change not their water at the muddy pool where tortoises bask in the sunshine, but at running brooks; talk not to friends, look not upon the face of a woman by the way, although she were as a gazelle, or as the maiden who when she walked through the fields the sheep stopped feeding to admire. Stop not, but run through day and night, pass through the Atlas at the Glaui; beware of frost, cover the bowl with thine own haik; upon the other side shield me the bowl from the Saharan sun, and drink not of the water if thou pass a day athirst when toiling through the sand. Break not the bowl, and see the fish arrive in Tafilet, and then present them, with this letter, to our lord. Allah be with you, and his Prophet; go, and above all things see thou breakest not the bowl." And Amarabat, after the manner of his kind, taking the bowl of gold fish, placed one hand upon his heart and said: "Inshallah, it shall be as thou hast said. God gives the feet and lungs. He also gives the luck upon the road."

So he passed out under the horseshoe arch, holding the bowl almost at arm's length so as not to touch his legs, and with the palmetto string by which he carried it, bound round with rags. The soldiers looked at him, but spoke not, and their eyes seemed to see far away, and to pass over all in the middle distance, though no doubt they marked the smallest detail of his gait and dress. He passed between the horses of the guard all standing nodding under the fierce sun, the reins tied to the cantles of their high red saddles, a boy in charge of every two or three: he passed beside the camels resting by the well, the donkeys standing dejected by the firewood they had brought: passed women, veiled white figures going to the baths; and passing underneath the lofty gateway of the town, exchanged a greeting with the half-mad, half-religious beggar just outside the walls, and then emerged upon the sandy road, between the aloe hedges, which skirts along the sea. So as he walked, little by little he fell into his stride; then got his second wind, and smoking now and then a pipe of hemp, began, as Arabs say, to eat the miles, his eyes fixed on the horizon, his stick stuck down between his shirt and back, the knob protruding over the left shoulder like the hilt of a two-handed sword. And still he held the precious bowl from Franguestan in which the golden fish swam to and fro, diving and circling in the sunlight, or flapped their tails to steady themselves as the water danced with the motion of his steps. Never before in his experience had he been charged with such a mission, never before been sent to stand before Allah's vicegerent upon earth. But still the strangeness of his business was what preoccupied him most. The fish like molten gold, the water to be changed only at running streams, the fish to be preserved from frost and sun; and then the bowl: had not the Khalifa said at the last, "Beware, break not the bowl"? So it appeared to him that most undoubtedly a charm was in the fish and in the bowl, for who sends common fish on such a journey through the land? Then he resolved at any hazard to bring them safe and keep the bowl intact, and trotting onward, smoked his hemp, and wondered why he of all men should have had the luck to bear the precious gift. He knew he kept his law, at least as far as a poor man can keep it, prayed when he thought of prayer, or was assailed by terror in the night alone upon the plains; fasted in Ramadan, although most of his life was one continual fast; drank of the shameful but seldom, and on the sly, so as to give offence to no believer, and seldom looked upon the face of the strange women, Daughters of the Illegitimate, whom Sidna Mohammed himself has said, avoid. But all these things he knew were done by many of the faithful, and so he did not set himself up as of exceeding virtue, but rather left the praise to God, who helped his slave with strength to keep his law. Then left off thinking, judging the matter was ordained, and trotted, trotted over the burning plains, the gold fish dancing in the water as the miles melted and passed away.

Duar and Kasbah, castles of the Caids, Arabs' black tents, suddra zaribas, camels grazing—antediluvian in appearance—on the little hills, the muddy streams edged all along the banks with oleanders, the solitary horsemen holding their long and brass-hooped guns like spears, the white-robed noiseless-footed travellers on the roads, the chattering storks upon the village mosques, the cow-birds sitting on the cattle in the fields—he saw, but marked not, as he trotted on. Day faded into night, no twilight intervening, and the stars shone out, Soheil and Rigel with Betelgeuse and Aldebaran, and the three bright lamps which the cursed Christians know as the Three Maries—called, he supposed, after the mother of their Prophet; and still he trotted on. Then by the side of a lone palm-tree springing up from a cleft in a tall rock, an island on the plain, he stopped to pray; and sleeping, slept but fitfully, the strangeness of the business making him wonder; and he who cavils over matters in the night can never rest, for thus the jackal and the hyena pass their nights talking and reasoning about the thoughts which fill their minds when men lie with their faces covered in their haiks, and after prayer sleep. Rising after an hour or two and going to the nearest stream, he changed the water of his fish, leaving a little in the bottom of the bowl, and dipping with his brass drinking-cup into the stream for fear of accidents. He passed the Kasbah of el Daudi, passed the land of the Rahamna, accursed folk always in *siba*, saw the great snowy wall of Atlas rise, skirted Marakesh, the Kutubieh, rising first from the plain and sinking last from sight as he approached the mountains and left the great white city sleeping in the plain.

Little by little the country altered as he ran: cool streams for muddy rivers, groves of almond trees, ashes and elms, with grape-vines binding them together as the liana binds the canela and the urunday in the dark forests of Brazil and Paraguay. At mid-day, when the sun was at its height, when locusts, whirring through the air, sank in the dust as flying-fish sink in the waves, when palm-trees seem to nod their heads, and lizards are abroad drinking the heat and basking in the rays, when the dry air shimmers, and sparks appear to dance before the traveller's eye, and a thin, reddish dust lies on the leaves, on clothes of men, and upon every hair of horses' coats, he reached a spring. A river springing from a rock, or issuing after running underground, had formed a little pond. Around the edge grew bulrushes, great catmace, water-soldiers, tall arums and metallic-looking sedge-grass, which gave an air as of an outpost of the tropics lost in the desert sand. Fish played beneath the rock where the stream issued, flitting to and fro, or hanging suspended for an instant in the clear stream, darted into the dark recesses of the sides; and in the middle of the pond enormous tortoises, horrid and antediluvian-looking, basked with their backs awash or raised their heads to snap at flies, and all about them hung a dark and fetid slime.

A troop of thin brown Arab girls filled their tall amphorae whilst washing in the pond. Placing his bowl of fish upon a jutting rock, the messenger drew near. "Gazelles," he said, "will one of you give me fresh water for the Sultan's golden fish?" Laughing and giggling, the girls drew near, looked at the bowl, had never seen such fish. "Allah is great; why do you not let them go in the pond and play a little with their brothers?" And Amarabat with a shiver answered, "Play, let them play! and if they come not back my life will answer for it." Fear fell upon the girls, and one advancing, holding the skirt of her long shift between her teeth to veil her face, poured water from her amphora upon the fish.

Then Amarabat, setting down her precious bowl, drew from his wallet a pomegranate and began to eat, and for a farthing buying a piece of bread from the women, was satisfied, and after smoking, slept, and dreamed he was approaching Tafilet; he saw the palm-trees rising from the sand; the gardens; all the oasis stretching beyond his sight; at the edge the Sultan's camp, a town of canvas, with the horses, camels, and the mules picketed, all in rows, and in the midst of the great *duar* the Sultan's tent, like a great palace all of canvas, shining in the sun. All this he saw, and saw himself entering the camp, delivering up his fish, perhaps admitted to the sacred tent, or at least paid by a vizier, as one who has performed his duty well. The slow match blistering his foot, he woke to find himself alone, the "gazelles" departed, and the sun shining on the bowl, making the fish appear more magical, more wondrous, brighter, and more golden than before.

And so he took his way along the winding Atlas paths, and slept at Demnats, then, entering the mountains, met long trains of travellers going to the south. Passing through groves of chestnuts, walnut-trees, and hedges thick with blackberries and travellers' joy, he climbed through vineyards rich with black Atlas grapes, and passed the flat mud-built Berber villages nestling against the rocks. Eagles flew by and moufflons gazed at him from the peaks, and from the thickets of lentiscus and dwarf arbutus wild boars appeared, grunted, and slowly walked across the path, and still he climbed, the icy wind from off the snow chilling him in his cotton shirt, for his warm Tadla haik was long ago wrapped round the bowl to shield the precious fish. Crossing the Wad Ghadat, the current to his chin, his bowl of fish held in one hand, he struggled on. The Berber tribesmen at Tetsula and Zarkten, hard-featured, shaved but for a chin-tuft, and robed in their *achnifs* with the curious eye woven in the skirt, saw he was a *rekass,* or thought the fish not worth their notice, so gave him a free road. Night caught him at the stone-built, antediluvian-looking Kasbah of the Glaui, perched in the eye of the pass, with the small plain of Teluet two thousand feet below. Off the high snow-peaks came a whistling wind, water froze solid in all the pots and pans, earthenware jars and bottles throughout the castle, save in the bowl which Amarabat, shivering and miserable, wrapped in his haik and held close to the embers, hearing the muezzin at each call to prayers; praying himself to keep awake so that his fish might live. Dawn saw him on the trail, the bowl wrapped in a woollen rag, and the fish fed with bread-crumbs, but himself hungry and his head swimming with want of sleep, with smoking *kief*, and with the bitter wind which from El Tisi N'Glaui flagellates the road. Right through the valley of Teluet he still kept on, and day and night still trotting, trotting on, changing his bowl almost instinctively from hand to hand, a broad leaf floating on the top to keep the water still, he left Agurzga, with its twin castles, Ghresat and Dads, behind. Then rapidly descending, in a day reached an oasis between Todghra and Ferkla, and rested at a village for the night. Sheltered by palm-trees and hedged round with cactuses and aloes, either to keep out thieves or as a symbol of the thorniness of life, the village lay, looking back on the white Atlas gaunt and mysterious, and on the other side towards the brown Sahara, land of the palm-tree (Belad-el-Jerid), the refuge of the true Ishmaelite; for in the desert, learning, good faith, and hospitality can still be found—at least, so Arabs say.

Orange and azofaifa trees, with almonds, sweet limes and walnuts, stood up against the waning light, outlined in the clear atmosphere almost so sharply as to wound the eye. Around the well goats and sheep lay, whilst a girl led a camel round the Noria track; women sat here and there and gossiped, with their tall earthenware jars stuck by the point into the ground, and waited for their turn, just as they did in the old times, so far removed from us, but which in Arab life is but as yesterday, when Jacob cheated Esau, and the whole scheme of Arab life was photographed for us by the writers of the Pentateuch. In fact, the self-same scene which has been acted every evening for two thousand years throughout North Africa, since the adventurous ancestors of the tribesmen of to-day left Hadrumut or Yemen, and upon which Allah looks down approvingly, as recognizing that the traditions of his first recorded life have been well kept. Next day he trotted through the barren plain of Seddat, the Jibel Saghra making a black line on the horizon to the south. Here Berber tribes sweep in their *razzias* like hawks; but who would plunder a rekass carrying a bowl of fish? Crossing the dreary plain and dreaming of his entry into Tafilet, which now was almost in his reach not two days distant, the sun beating on his head, the water almost boiling in the bowl, hungry and footsore, and in the state betwixt waking and sleep into which those who smoke hemp on journeys often get, he branched away upon a trail leading towards the south. Between the oases of Todghra and Ferkla, nothing but stone and sand, black stones on yellow sand; sand, and yet more sand, and then again stretches of blackish rocks with a suddra bush or two, and here and there a colocynth, bitter and beautiful as love or life, smiling up at the traveller from amongst the stones. Towards midday the path led towards a sandy tract all overgrown with sandarac bushes and crossed by trails of jackals and hyenas, then it quite disappeared, and Amarabat waking from his dream saw he was lost. Like a good shepherd, his first thought was for his fish; for he imagined the last few hours of sun had made them faint, and one of them looked heavy and swam sideways, and the rest kept rising to the surface in an uneasy way. Not for a moment was Amarabat frightened, but looked about for some known landmark, and finding none started to go back on his trail. But to his horror the wind which always sweeps across the Sahara had covered up his tracks, and on the stony paths which he had passed his feet had left no prints. Then Amarabat, the first moments of despair passed by, took a long look at the horizon, tightened his belt, pulled up his slipper heels, covered his precious bowl with a corner of his robe, and started doggedly back upon the road he thought he traversed on the deceitful path. How long he trotted, what he endured, whether the fish died first, or if he drank, or, faithful to the last, thirsting met death, no one can say. Most likely wandering in the waste of sandhills and of suddra bushes he stumbled on, smoking his hashish while it lasted, turning to Mecca at the time of prayer, and trotting on more feebly (for he was born to run), till he sat down beneath the sun-dried bushes where the Shinghiti on his Mehari found him dead beside the trail. Under a stunted sandarac tree, the head turned to the east, his body lay, swollen and distorted by the pangs of thirst, the tongue protruding rough as a parrot's, and beside him lay the seven golden fish, once bright and shining as the pure gold when the goldsmith pours it molten from his pot, but now turned black and bloated, stiff, dry, and dead. Life the mysterious, the mocking, the inscrutable, unseizable, the uncomprehended essence of nothing and of everything, had fled, both from the faithful messenger and from his fish. But the Khalifa's parting caution had been well obeyed, for by the tree, unbroken, the crystal bowl still glistened beautiful as gold, in the fierce rays of the Saharan sun.

A Hegira

The giant cypresses, tall even in the time of Montezuma, the castle of Chapultepec upon its rock (an island in the plain of Mexico), the panorama of the great city backed by the mountain range; the two volcanoes, the Popocatepetl and the Istacihuatl, and the lakes; the tigers in their cages, did not interest me so much as a small courtyard, in which, ironed and guarded, a band of Indians of the Apache tribe were kept confined. Six warriors, a woman and a boy, captured close to Chihuahua, and sent to Mexico, the Lord knows why; for generally an Apache captured was shot at once, following the frontier rule, which without difference of race was held on both sides of the Río Grande, that a good Indian must needs be dead.

Silent and stoical the warriors sat, not speaking once in a whole day, communicating but by signs; naked except the breech-clout; their eyes apparently opaque, and looking at you without sight, but seeing everything; and their demeanour less reassuring than that of the tigers in the cage hard by. All could speak Spanish if they liked, some a word or two of English, but no one heard them say a word in either tongue. I asked the nearest if he was a Mescalero, and received the answer: *"Mescalero-hay,"* and for a moment a gleam shone through their eyes, but vanished instantly, as when the light dies out of the wire in an electric lamp. The soldier at the gate said they were "brutes"; all sons of dogs, infidels, and that for his part he could not see why the *Gobierno* went to the expense of keeping them alive. He thought they had no sense; but in that showed his own folly, and acted after the manner of the half-educated man the whole world over, who knowing he can read and write thinks that the savage who cannot do so is but a fool; being unaware that, in the great book known as the world, the savage often is the better scholar of the two.

But five-and-twenty years ago the Apache nation, split into its chief divisions of Mescaleros, Jicarillas, Coyoteros, and Lipanes, kept a great belt of territory almost five hundred miles in length, and of about thirty miles in breadth, extending from the bend of the Río Gila to El Paso, in a perpetual war. On both sides of the Río Grande no man was safe; farms were deserted, cattle carried off, villages built by the Spaniards, and with substantial brick-built churches, mouldered into decay; mines were unworkable, and horses left untended for a moment were driven off in open day; so bold the thieves, that at one time they had a settled month for plundering, which they called openly the Moon of the Mexicans, though they did not on that account suspend their operations at other seasons of the year. Cochise and Mangas-Coloradas, Naked Horse, Cuchillo Negro, and others of their chiefs, were once far better known upon the frontiers than the chief senators of the congresses of either of the two republics; and in some instances these chiefs showed an intelligence, knowledge of men and things, which in another sphere would certainly have raised them high in the estimation of mankind.

The Shis-Inday (the people of the woods), their guttural

language, with its curious monosyllable *hay* which they tacked on to everything, as *oro-hay* and *plata-hay;* their strange democracy, each man being chief of himself, and owing no allegiance to any one upon the earth; all now have almost passed away, destroyed and swallowed up by the *"Inday pindah lichoyi"* (the men of the white eyes), as they used to call the Americans and all those northerners who ventured into their territory to look for "yellow iron." I saw no more of the Apaches, and except once, never again met any one of them; but as I left the place the thought came to my mind, if any of them succeed in getting out, I am certain that the six or seven hundred miles between them and their country will be as nothing to them, and that their journey thither will be marked with blood.

At Huehuetoca I joined the mule-train, doing the twenty miles which in those days was all the extent of railway in the country to the north, and lost my pistol in a crowd just as I stepped into the train, some *lepero* having abstracted it out of my belt when I was occupied in helping five strong men to get my horse into a cattle-truck. From Huehuetoca we marched to Tula, and there camped for the night, sleeping in a *mesón* built like an Eastern fondak round a court, and with a well for watering the beasts in the centre of the yard. I strolled about the curious town, in times gone by the Aztec capital, looked at the churches, built like fortresses, and coming back to the mesón before I entered the cell-like room without a window, and with a plaster bench on which to spread one's saddle and one's rugs, I stopped to talk with a knot of travellers feeding their animals on barley and chopped straw, grouped round a fire, and the whole scene lit up and rendered Rembrandtesque by the fierce glow of an ocote torch. So talking of the Alps and Apennines, or, more correctly, speaking of the Sierra Madre, and the mysterious region known as the Bolsón de Mapimi, a district in those days as little known as is the Sus to-day, a traveller drew near. Checking his horse close by the fire, and getting off it gingerly, for it was almost wild, holding the hair *mecate* in his hand, he squatted down, the horse snorting and hanging back, and setting rifle and machete jingling upon the saddle, he began to talk.

"*Ave María purísima*, had we heard the news?" What! a new revolution? Had Lerdo de Tejada reappeared again? or had Cortinas made another raid on Brownsville? the Indios Bravos harried Chihuahua? or had the silver "conduct" coming from the mines been robbed? "Nothing of this, but a voice ran *(coría una voz)* that the Apache infidels confined in the courtyard of the castle of Chapultepec had broken loose. Eight of them, six warriors, a woman and a boy, had slipped their fetters, murdered two of the guard, and were supposed to be somewhere not far from Tula, and," as he thought, "making for the Bolsón de Mapimi, the deserts of the Río Gila, or the recesses of the mountains of the Santa Rosa range."

Needless to say this put all in the mesón almost beside themselves; for the terror that the Indians inspired was at that time so real, that had the eight forlorn and helpless infidels appeared I verily believe they would have killed us all. Not that we were not brave, well armed—in fact, all loaded down with arms, carrying rifles and pistols, swords stuck between our saddle-girths, and generally so fortified as to resemble walking arsenals. But valour is a thing of pure convention, and these men who would have fought like lions against marauders of their own race, scarce slept that night for thinking on the dangers which they ran by the reported presence of those six naked men. The night passed by without alarm, as was to be expected, seeing that the courtyard wall of the mesón was at least ten feet high, and the gate solid *ahuehuete* clamped with iron, and padlocked like a jail. At the first dawn, or rather at the first false dawn, when the fallacious streaks of pink flash in the sky and fade again to night, all were afoot. Horsemen rode out, sitting erect in their peaked saddles, toes stuck out and thrust into their curiously stamped toe-leathers; their *chaparejos* giving to their legs a look of being cased in armour, their *poblano* hats, with bands of silver or of tinsel, balanced like halos on their heads.

Long trains of donkeys, driven by Indians dressed in leather, and bareheaded, after the fashion of their ancestors, crawled through the gate laden with *pulque*, and now and then a single Indian followed by his wife set off on foot, carrying a crate of earthenware by a broad strap depending from his head. Our caravan, consisting of six two-wheeled mule-carts, drawn by a team of six or sometimes eight gaily-harnessed mules, and covered with a tilt made from the *istle,* creaked through the gate. The great mesón remained deserted, and by degrees, as a ship leaves the coast, we struck into the wild and stony desert country, which, covered with a whitish dust of alkali, makes Tula an oasis; then the great church sank low, and the tall palm-trees seemed to grow shorter; lastly church, palms and towers, and the green fields planted with aloes, blended together and sank out of sight, a faint white misty spot marking their whereabouts, till at last it too faded and melted into the level plain.

Travellers in a perpetual stream we met journeying to Mexico, and every now and then passed a straw-thatched *jacal,* where women sat selling *atole,* that is a kind of stirabout of pine-nut meal and milk, and dishes seasoned hot with red pepper, with tortillas made on the *metate* of the Aztecs, to serve as bread and spoons. The infidels, it seemed, had got ahead of us, and when we slept had been descried making towards the north; two of them armed with bows which they had roughly made with sticks, the string twisted out of istle, and the rest with clubs, and what astonished me most was that behind them trotted a white dog. Outside San Juan del Río, which we reached upon the second day, it seemed that in the night the homing Mescaleros had stolen a horse, and two of them mounting upon him had ridden off, leaving the rest of the forlorn and miserable band behind. How they had lived so far in the scorched alkali-covered plains, how they managed to conceal themselves by day, or how they steered by night, no one could tell; for the interior Mexican knows nothing of the desert craft, and has no idea that there is always food of some kind for an Apache, either by digging roots, snaring small animals, or at the last resort by catching locusts or any other insect he can find. Nothing so easy as to conceal themselves; for amongst grass eight or nine inches high, they drop, and in an instant, even as you look, are lost to sight, and if hard pressed sometimes escape attention by standing in a cactus grove, and stretching out their arms, look so exactly like the plant that you may pass close to them and be unaware, till their bow twangs, and an obsidian-headed arrow whistles through the air.

Our caravan rested a day outside San Juan del Río to shoe the mules, repair the harness, and for the muleteers to go to mass or visit the poblana girls, who with flowers in their hair leaned out of every balcony of the half-Spanish, half-Oriental-looking town, according to their taste. Not that the halt lost time, for travellers all know that "to hear mass and to give barley to your beasts loses no tittle of the day."

San Juan, the river almost dry, and trickling thirstily under its red stone bridges; the fields of aloes, the poplars, and the stunted palms; its winding street in which the houses, overhanging, almost touch; its population, which seemed to pass their time lounging wrapped in striped blankets up against the walls, was left behind. The pulque-aloes and the sugar-canes grew scarcer, the road more desolate as we emerged into the *tierra fría* of the central plain, and all the time the Sierra Madre, jagged and menacing, towered in the west. In my mind's eye I saw the Mescaleros trotting like wolves all through the night along its base, sleeping by day in holes, killing a sheep or goat when chance occurred, and following one another silent and stoical in their tramp towards the north.

Days followed days as in a ship at sea; the waggons rolling on across the plains; and I jogging upon my horse, half sleeping in the sun, or stretched at night half dozing on a tilt, almost lost count of time. Somewhere between San Juan del Río and San Luis Potosí we learned two of the Indians had been killed, but that the four remaining were still pushing onward, and in a little while we met a body of armed men carrying two ghastly heads tied by their scalp-locks to the saddle-bow. Much did the slayers vaunt their prowess; telling how in a wood at break of day they had fallen in with all the Indians seated round a fire, and that whilst the rest fled, two had sprung on them, as they said, "after the fashion of wild beasts, armed one with a stick, and the other with a stone, and by God's grace," and here the leader crossed himself, "their aim had been successful, and the two sons of dogs had fallen, but most unfortunately the rest during the fight had managed to escape."

San Luis Potosí, the rainless city, once world-renowned for wealth, and even now full of fine buildings, churches and palaces, and with a swarming population of white-clothed Indians squatting to sell their trumpery in the great market-square, loomed up amongst its fringe of gardens, irrigated lands, its groves of pepper-trees, its palms, its wealth of flowering shrubs; its great white domes, giving an air of Bagdad or of Fez, shone in the distance, then grew nearer, and at last swallowed us up, as wearily we passed through the outskirts of the town, and halted underneath the walls.

The city, then an oasis in the vast plateau of Anáhuac (now but a station on a railway-line), a city of enormous distances, of gurgling water led in stucco channels by the side of every street, of long expanses of *adobe* walls, of immense plazas, of churches and of bells, of countless convents; hedged in by mountains to the west, mouth of the *tierra caliente* to the east, and to the north the stopping-place for the long trains of waggons carrying cotton from the States; wrapped in a mist as of the Middle Ages, lay sleeping in the sun. On every side the plain lapped like an ocean, and the green vegetation round the town stopped so abruptly that you could step almost at once from fertile meadows into a waste of whitish alkali.

Above the town, in a foothill of the Sierra Madre about three leagues away, is situated the "Enchanted City," never yet fouled by the foot of man, but yet existent, and believed in by all those who follow that best part of history, the traditions which have come down to us from the times when men were wise, and when imagination governed judgment, as it should do to-day, being the noblest faculty of the human mind. Either want of time, or that belittling education from which few can escape, prevented me from visiting the place. Yet I still think if rightly sought the city will be found, and I feel sure the Mescaleros passed the night not far from it, and perhaps looking down upon San Luis Potosí cursed it, after the fashion that the animals may curse mankind for its injustice to them.

Tired of its squares, its long dark streets, its hum of people; and possessed perhaps with that nostalgia of the desert which comes so soon to all who once have felt its charm when cooped in bricks, we set our faces northward about an hour before the day, passed through the gates and rolled into the plains. The mules well rested shook their bells, the leagues soon dropped behind, the muleteers singing "La Pasadita," or an interminable song about a "Gachupin"[1] who loved a nun.

The Mescaleros had escaped our thoughts—that is, the muleteers thought nothing of them; but I followed their every step, saw them crouched round their little fire, roasting the roots of wild *mescal;* marked them upon the march in single file, their eyes fixed on the plain, watchful and silent as they were phantoms gliding to the north.

Crossing a sandy tract, the Capataz, who had long lived in the Pimeria Alta and amongst the Maricopas on the Gila, drew up his horse and pointing to the ground said, *"Viva México!*—look at these footmarks in the sand. They are the infidels; see where the men have trod; here is the woman's print and this the boy's. Look how their toes are all turned in, unlike the tracks of Christians. This trail is a day old, and yet how fresh! See where the boy has stumbled—thanks to the Blessed Virgin they must all be tired, and praise to God will die upon the road, either by hunger or some Christian hand." All that he spoke of was no doubt visible to him, but through my want of faith, or perhaps lack of experience, I saw but a faint trace of naked foototops in the sand. Such as they were, they seemed the shadow of a ghost, unstable and unreal, and struck me after the fashion that it strikes one when a man holds up a cane and tells you gravely, without a glimmering of the strangeness of the fact, that it came from Japan, actually grew there, and had leaves and roots, and was as little thought of as a mere ash-plant growing in a copse.

At an hacienda upon the road, just where the trail leads off upon one hand to Matehuala, and on the other to Río Verde, and the hot countries of the coast, we stopped to pass the hottest hours in sleep. All was excitement; men came in, their horses flecked with foam; others were mounting, and all armed to the teeth, as if the Yankees had crossed the Río Grande, and were marching on the place. *"Los Indios! si, señor,"* they had been seen, only last night, but such the valour of the people of the place, they had passed on doing no further damage than to kill a lamb. No chance of sleep in such a turmoil of alarm; each man had his own plan, all talked at once, most of them were half drunk, and when our Capataz asked dryly if they had thought of following the trail, a silence fell on all. By this time, owing to the horsemen galloping about, the trail was cut on every side, and to have followed it would have tried the skill of an Apache tracker; but just then upon the plain a cloud of dust was seen. Nearer it came, and then out of the midst of it horses appeared, arms flashed, and when nearing the place five or six men galloped up to the walls, and stopped their horses with a jerk. "What news? have you seen anything of the Apaches?" and the chief rider of the gallant band, getting off slowly, and fastening up his horse, said, with an air of dignity, "At the *encrucijada*, four leagues along the road, you will find one of them. We came upon him sitting on a stone, too tired to move, called on him to surrender, but Indians have no sense, so he came at us tired as he was, and we, being valiant, fired, and he fell dead. Then, that the law should be made manifest to all, we hung his body by the feet to a huisache tree." Then compliments broke out and *"Viva los valientes!" "Viva México!" "Mueran los Indios salvajes!"* and much of the same sort, whilst the five valiant men modestly took a drink, saying but little, for true courage does not show itself in talk.

Leaving the noisy crew drinking confusion to their enemies, we rolled into the plain. Four dusty leagues, and the huisache tree growing by four cross trails came into sight. We neared it, and to a branch, naked except his breech-clout, covered with bullet-wounds, we saw the Indian hang. Half-starved he looked, and so reduced that from the bullet-holes but little blood had run; his feet were bloody, and his face hanging an inch or two above the ground distorted; flies buzzed about him, and in the sky a faint black line on the horizon showed that the vultures had already scented food.

We left the nameless warrior hanging on his tree, and took our way across the plain, well pleased both with the "valour" of his slayers and the position of affairs in general in the world at large. Right up and down the Río Grande on both sides for almost a thousand miles the lonely cross upon some river-side, near to some thicket, or out in the wide plain, most generally is lettered "Killed by the Apaches," and in the game they played so long, and still held trumps in at the time I write of, they, too, paid for all errors, in their play, by death. But still it seemed a pity, savage as they were, that so much cunning, such stoical indifference to both death and life, should always finish as the warrior whom I saw hang by the feet from the huisache, just where the road to Matehuala bifurcates, and the trail breaks off to El Jarral. And so we took our road, passed La Parida, Matehuala, El Catorce, and still the sterile plateau spread out like a vast sea, the sparse and stunted bushes in the constant mirage looming at times like trees, at others seeming just to float above the sand; and as we rolled along, the mules struggling and straining in the whitish dust, we seemed to lose all trace of the Apaches; and at the lone hacienda or rare villages no one had heard of them, and the mysterious hegira of the party, now reduced to three, left no more traces of its passing than water which has closed upon the passage of a fish.

Gómez Farias, Parras, El Llano de la Guerra, we passed alternately, and at length Saltillo came in sight, its towers standing up upon the plain after the fashion of a light-house in the sea; the bull-ring built under the Viceroys looking like a fort; and then the plateau of Anáhuac finished abruptly, and from the ramparts of the willow-shaded town the great green plains stretched out towards Texas in a vast panorama; whilst upon the west in the dim distance frowned the serrated mountains of Santa Rosa, and further still the impenetrable fastnesses of the Bolsón de Mapimi.

Next day we took the road for Monterey, descending in a day by the rough path known as *la cuesta de los fierros,* from the cold plateau to a land of palms, of cultivation, orange-groves, of fruit-trees, olive-gardens, a balmy air filled with the noise of running waters; and passing underneath the Cerro de la Silla which dominates the town, slept peacefully far from all thoughts of Indians and of perils of the road, in the great caravansary which at that time was the chief glory of the town of Monterey. The city with its shady streets, its alameda planted with palm-trees, and its plaza all decorated with stuccoed plaster seats painted pale pink, and upon which during both day and night half of the population seemed to lounge, lay baking in the sun.

Great teams of waggons driven by Texans creaked through the streets, the drivers dressed in a *défroque* of old town clothes, often a worn frock-coat and rusty trousers stuffed into cowboy boots, the whole crowned with an ignominious battered hat, and looking, as the Mexicans observed, like *"pantomimas, que salen en las fiestas."* Mexicans from down the coast, from Tamaulipas, Tuxpan, Vera Cruz and Guatzecoalcos ambled along on horses all ablaze with silver; and to complete the picture, a tribe of Indians, the Kickapoos, who had migrated from the north, and who occasionally rode through the town in single file, their rifles in their hands, and looking at the shops half longingly, half frightened, passed along without a word.

But all the varied peoples, the curious half-wild, half-patriarchal life, the fruits and flowers, the strangeness of the place, could not divert my thoughts from the three lone pathetic figures, followed by their dog, which in my mind's eye I saw making northward, as a wild goose finds its path in spring, leaving no traces of its passage by the way. I wondered what they thought of, how they looked upon the world, if they respected all they saw of civilized communities upon their way, or whether they pursued their journey like a horse let loose returning to his birthplace, anxious alone about arriving at the goal. So Monterey became a memory; the Cerro de la Silla last vanishing, when full five leagues upon the road. The dusty plains all white with alkali, the grey-green sage-bushes, the salt and crystal-looking rivers, the Indians bending under burdens, and the women sitting at the cross roads selling tortillas—all now had changed. Through oceans of tall grass, by muddy rivers in which alligators basked, by *bayous, resacas,* and by bottoms of alluvial soil, in which grew cotton-woods, black-jack, and post-oak, with gigantic willows; through countless herds of half-wild horses, lighting the landscape with their colours, and through a rolling prairie with vast horizons bounded by faint blue mountain chains, we took our way. Out of the thickets of *mezquite* wild boars peered upon the path; rattlesnakes sounded their note of warning or lay basking in the sun; at times an antelope bounded across our track, and the rare villages were fortified with high mud walls, had gates, and sometimes drawbridges, for all the country we were passing through was subject to invasions of *los Indios Bravos,* and no one rode a mile without the chance of an attack. When travellers met they zigzagged to and fro like battleships in the old days striving to get the "weather gauge," holding their horses tightly by the head, and interchanging salutations fifty yards away, though if they happened to be Texans and Mexicans they only glared, or perhaps yelled an obscenity at one another in their different tongues. Advertisements upon the trees informed the traveller that the place to stop at was the "Old Buffalo Camp" in San Antonio, setting forth its whisky, its perfect safety both for man and beast, and adding curtly it was only a short four hundred miles away. Here for the first time in our journey we sent out a rider about half-a-mile ahead to scan the route, ascend the little hills, keep a sharp eye on "Indian sign," and give us warning by a timely shot, all to dismount, corral the waggons, and be prepared for an attack of Indians, or of the roaming bands of rascals who like pirates wandered on the plains. Dust made us anxious, and smoke ascending in the distance set us all wondering if it was Indians, or a shepherd's fire; at halting time no one strayed far from camp, and we sat eating with our rifles by our sides, whilst men on horseback rode round the mules, keeping them well in sight, as shepherds watch their sheep. About two leagues from Juarez a traveller bloody with spurring passed us carrying something in his hand; he stopped and held out a long arrow with an obsidian head, painted in various colours, and feathered in a peculiar way. A consultation found it to be "Apache," and the man galloped on to take it to the governor of the place to tell him Indians were about, or, as he shouted (following the old Spanish catchword), "there were Moors upon the coast."

Juarez we slept at, quite secure within the walls; started at daybreak, crossing the swiftly-running river just outside the town, at the first streak of light; journeyed all day, still hearing nothing of the retreating Mescaleros, and before evening reached Las Navas, which we found astir, all lighted up, and knots of people talking excitedly, whilst in the plaza the whole population seemed to be afoot. At the long wooden tables set about with lights, where in a Mexican town at sundown an al fresco meal of kid stewed in red pepper, tamales and tortillas, is always laid, the talk was furious, and each man gave his opinion at the same time, after the fashion of the Russian Mir, or as it may be that we shall yet see done during debates in Parliament, so that all men may have a chance to speak, and yet escape the ignominy of their words being caught, set down, and used against them, after the present plan. The Mescaleros had been seen passing about a league outside the town. A shepherd lying hidden, watching his sheep, armed with a rifle, had spied them, and reported that they had passed close to him; the woman coming last and carrying in her arms a little dog; and he "thanked God and all His holy saints who had miraculously preserved his life." After the shepherd's story, in the afternoon firing had been distinctly heard towards the small rancho of Las Crucecitas, which lay about three leagues further on upon the road. All night the din of talk went on, and in the morning when we started on our way, full half the population went with us to the gate, all giving good advice; to keep a good look-out, if we saw dust to be certain it was Indians driving the horses stolen from Las Crucecitas, then to get off at once, corral the waggons, and above all to put our trust in God. This we agreed to do, but wondered why out of so many valiant men not one of them proffered assistance, or volunteered to mount his horse and ride with us along the dangerous way.

The road led upwards towards some foothills, set about with scrubby palms; not fifteen miles away rose the dark mountains of the Santa Rosa chain, and on a little hill the rancho stood, flat-roofed and white, and seemingly not more than a short league away, so clear the light, and so immense the scale of everything upon the rolling plain. I knew that in the mountains the three Indians were safe, as the whole range was Indian territory; and as I saw them struggling up the slopes, the little dog following them footsore, hanging down its head, or carried as the shepherd said in the "she-devil's" arms, I wished them luck after their hegira, planned with such courage, carried out so well, had ended, and they were back again amongst the tribe.

Just outside Crucecitas we met a Texan who, as he told us, owned the place, and lived in "kornkewbinage with a native gal" called, as he said, "Pastory," who it appeared of all the females he had ever met was the best hand to bake "tortillers," and whom, had she not been a Catholic, he would have made his wife. All this without a question on our part, and sitting sideways on his horse, scanning the country from the corner of his eye. He told us that he had "had right smart of an Indian trouble here yesterday just about afternoon. Me and my 'vaquerys' were around looking for an estray horse, just six of us, when close to the ranch we popped kermash right upon three red devils, and opened fire at once. I hed a Winchester, and at the first fire tumbled the buck; he fell right in his tracks, and jest as I was taking off his scalp, I'm doggoned if the squaw and the young devil didn't come at us jest like grizzly bars. Wal, yes, killed 'em, o' course, and anyhow the young 'un would have growed up; but the squaw I'm sort of sorry about. I never could bear to kill a squaw, though I've often seen it done. Naow here's the all-firedest thing yer ever heard; jes' as I was turning the bodies over with my foot a little Indian dog flies at us like a 'painter,' the varmint, the condemndest little buffler I ever struck. I was for shootin' him, but 'Pastory'—that's my 'kornkewbyne'—she up and says it was a shame. Wal, we had to bury them, for dead Injun stinks worse than turkey-buzzard, and the dodgasted little dog is sitting on the grave, 'pears like he's froze, leastwise he hasn't moved since sun-up, when we planted the whole crew."

Under a palm-tree not far from the house the Indians' grave was dug, upon it, wretched and draggled, sat the little dog. "Pastory" tried to catch it all day long, being kind-hearted though a "kornkewbyne"; but, failing, said "God was not willing," and retired into the house. The hours seemed days in the accursed place till the sun rose, gilding the unreached Santa Rosa mountains, and bringing joy into the world. We harnessed up the mules, and started silently out on the lonely road; turning, I checked my horse, and began moralizing on all kinds of things; upon tenacity of purpose, the futility of life, and the inexorable fate which mocks mankind, making all effort useless, whilst still urging us to strive. Then the grass rustled, and across an open space a small white object trotted, looking furtively around, threw up its head and howled, ran to and fro as if it sought for something, howled dismally again, and after scratching in the ground, squatted dejectedly on the fresh-turned-up earth which marked the Indians' grave.

Note

1. It had a chorus reflecting upon convent discipline:

"For though the convent rule was strict and tight,
Sho had hor quito and her ontranoo by night."

[C. G.]

The Pyramid

Fat, meretricious women in evening gowns had sung their ballads, their patter songs, their patriotic airs, in sentimental or in alcoholic tones. Comedians in checked clothes and sandy wigs, adorned with great red whiskers, and holding either short canes or bulgy umbrellas, had made the whole "Pretoria" laugh, till the vast music hall seemed to rock, as a volcano in activity is shaken with its interior fire.

Women and men had hung head downward from trapezes, had swung across the audience and been caught by the feet or hands by other "artistes" swinging to meet them suspended by one foot. Tottering and miserably anthropomorphous dogs had fired off cannons, and cats had tremblingly got into baskets with fox terriers; a skinny, sallow French *divette* had edified the audience with indecencies, rendered quite tolerable because half understood. Men dressed in evening clothes had bawled about the empire, holding a champagne glass in one hand whilst with their other hand they pressed a satin opera hat against their epigastrum; and as the songs became more patriotic or more obscene, and as each trick of the equilibrists, trapezists, wire-walkers and the rest became more dangerous, the public—the respectable, the discerning, the sovereign public—had testified its joy in shouts, in clappings, and in stampings, and by thumping with its sticks and umbrellas on the floor.

Over the auditorium, tobacco smoke hung like a vulgar incense in the shoddy temple of some false and tinsel god. In the great lounges the women sat at tables, dressed in a caricature of the prevailing styles; their boots too pointed, their gowns too tightly laced, their hair too curled or too much flattened to the head; and talked to youths in evening dress; to men who had the mark of husbands out on strike; to padded and painted elders, who whispered in their ears and plied them with champagne. Others who, out of luck, had found no man to hire them, walked up and down in pairs, pushing against such men as looked like customers, laughing and joking to one another, or singly stalked about, bored and dejected, and their legs trailing along imprisoned in their rustling skirts, enduring all the martyrdom of the perpetual walking which is the curse entailed upon their class. Behind the bars, the barmaids, painted and curled, kept up a running fire of half indecent chaff with the intelligent consumers of American drinks, of whisky-splits, or lemon-squashes, returning change for half a sovereign if the drinker was too far gone in liquor to observe it was a sovereign he put down.

Cadaverous and painted youths, with hot-house flowers in their buttonholes, paraded up and down, as it seemed for no particular purpose, speaking to no one, but occasionally exchanging glances with the women as they passed upon their beat.

In fact, the great, the generous, public was represented in all its phases, of alcoholic, of bestial, brutal, lustful, stupid, and of commonplace. Yet each one knew he was a part and parcel of a great empire, and was well convinced that in his person in some mysterious way he made for righteousness. The soldier sitting with his sweetheart in the gallery; the rich young idler about town, with his dressed-up and be-jewelled mistress in the stalls; the betting men—made, it is well not to forget, in their creator's image—each, all, and every one, knew he was not as men of other nations, but in some way was better, purer, and more manly than the best citizen of any foreign race. And so they sat, confident that all the performers, of whatever class, lived on their approbation, as it was certain they existed on their entrance fee. No trick so dangerous as to awake their pity, no song quite vile enough to make them feel ashamed to see a man or woman publicly prostitute their talents for their sport. Brutal, yet kindly folk they were, quite unappreciative of anything but fun and coarse indecency; of feats on which the performer's life hung on a hair; but still idealistic, sentimental souls, easily moved to tears with claptrap sentiment, and prone to clench their fists, and feel an ardour as of William Tell, when from the stage a man waved a small Union Jack or sang of Britain and her Colonies, ending each verse of his patriotic chant with a refrain of "hands across the sea."

And so the evening wore away. The performer on the fiddle with one string was suceeded by the quick-change "artiste," who in an instant appeared as a life-guardsman, walked across the stage and came on as a ballet dancer or an archdeacon, a costermonger, or lady from a cathedral city, and still in every change of costume looked the clever humorous Italian that he was.

Footmen in gorgeous liveries removed the numbers from the wings, and stuck up others, doing their duty proudly, being well aware their noble calves saved them from ridicule. The orchestra boomed and thumped through German waltzes, popular songs, and Spanish music, with the Spanish rhythm all left out, so that it sounded just as common as it were made at home.

Between eleven and twelve, turn number seventeen, the

début of "La Famiglia Sinigaglia" stood announced. Carpenters came and went upon the stage, and reared a kind of scaffold some fifteen feet in height. Then the "Famiglia Sinigaglia" came upon the scene—the father, mother, two children under ten years old, and five tall girls ranging from sixteen up to five-and-twenty years. The father, of some fifty years of age, was stout and muscular, his eyes as black as sloes, moustache and chin-tuft waxed to points, hair gone upon the crown, which shone like ivory, but still clinging to the occiput like sea weed to a rock. Those who had been responsible for what they did had called him at his baptism Annibale, which name he bore as conscious of the responsibility it laid on him, half modestly and half defiantly, with a perception of the ludicrous in life which yet did not distract him an iota from his profession, which he esteemed the noblest in the world.

"*Altro Signore,* ours is reality, not like the painters and the poets, with the musicians and the actors, who, if they miss their tip, can try again; but we, *per Bacco,* when we miss, straight to the *Campo Santo, Corpo del Bambin.*"

The mother, stout and merry-looking, was flaccid from the waist upwards, and had legs as of a mastodon, into the skin of which her high blue satin boots seemed to embed themselves, and to become incorporated. The children passed from hand to hand like cricket balls, being projected from Annibale to his wife La Sinigaglia, behind his back, flying between his legs, alighting on her shoulders or her head like birds upon a bough. Watching this tumbling stood the five daughters in a row. All dressed in tights, with trunks so short, they seemed to cut into their flesh, and so cut open on the hips, that it seemed marvellous what kept them in their place. They were all muscular, especially the eldest, who bid fair to be a rival to her mother in flesh and merriness; her eyes, roving about the theatre, smiled pleasantly when they met anyone's, after the fashion of a Newfoundland dog. The others, slighter

in form, were replicas of her at stated intervals. The
youngest, thinner than the rest, seemed less good-natured,
and with her brown bare arms folded across her chest
stood rather sullenly looking at nothing, smoothing down
her tights, crossing her feet, and then uncrossing them,
and now and then, raising her head, looked out into the
theatre, half frightened, half defiantly. The tumbling of
the children done, the father lying on his back threw the
fattest of his girls from his feet towards the mother who
caught her with her feet right in the middle of the back,
after a somersault. The public knowing the trick was
dangerous applauded joyfully, and then the five tall girls
stepped out to build the pyramid. The eldest, straddling her
legs, folded her arms, after saluting right and left with the
te morituri gesture, which perhaps the modern acrobat has
had straight from the gladiator. Her sister climbed upon
her shoulders and stood upright, waving her arms a minute, smiling as the applause broke out from the spectators
in the theatre. Taking a lace-edged pocket-handkerchief
from some mysterious hiding place, she wiped her hands,
and bending down signed to another sister, who clam-
bered up, and in her turn stood on her shoulders. The
fourth succeeded, and as they stood, the lowest sister
staggered a little, and took a step to get her balance,
making the pyramid all rock, and causing Annibale to swear
beneath his breath, and mutter to his wife.

"*Su Gigia,*" and the fifth sister ran up the staging like a
monkey, and stepping from it stood on the topmost sister's
hands in the attitude of John of Bologna's Mercury, one
arm uplifted, and her eyes turned upwards to the roof.
The supporting sister staggered a pace or two into the
middle of the stage, the perspiration dripping from her
face, and then saluted cautiously with her right hand, and
the three others broke into a smile which they had learned
together with their tricks.

The audience burst into applause, Annibale and La

Sinigaglia looked at each other with content, knowing their turn had taken on, and from the top of the high pyramid the youngest sister glared at the applauders with hatred and contempt, opening her eyes so that the pupils almost seemed to burst; but as she glared the public kept applauding, being aware that acrobats live on its breath, and counting it as righteousness they were not stinted in their food.

A Yorkshire Tragedy

It was an idle day, in every street men stood about and talked in whispers, or squatting on their heels as miners do, accustomed to a narrow seam, stared blankly, as they smoked their short clay pipes. A pall of coal-dust almost obscured the sky, and on the grass and leaves of trees, on slates and window panes, and on the tops of posts, it formed a sort of frost, but black and hideous as of a world decayed.

It clung to wires and made them furry as they were caterpillars, and upon hair and beards it stuck about the roots beyond the power of any soap to clean. Round eyelashes it lay like paint, making the eyes seem sunken and still giving them a brilliancy which looked unnatural.

The village where the miners lived was built of dark grey stone and in a series of long rows divided by partitions, each section with its water-butt, its low stone wall in front, and with a gate which as a general rule stood open, having lost the hinges, or was tied up with string.

The shops were little stores in which were sold grey flannel shirts and boots with wooden soles, cheap bacon and strong cheese, currants and Abernethy biscuits, sized calicoes and twist tobacco, with clay pipes, each with its perforated cap of tin kept in its place by a thin chain which dangled from the stem.

The streets were worn into black waves by heavy carts, and the thick mud, summer or winter, never seemed to dry. Children and whippets ran about the place: the former playing at old-fashioned games, as tig and hopscotch, long forgotten in the south; the latter walking about with dignity, as if aware of the consideration they enjoyed, but not presuming on it, for every child wore wooden clogs and used them with a skill only long practice gives.

Chapels and drink-shops elbowed each other in the town, and a small park in which grew stunted trees that sprang from earth that looked like scoria of a coalpit was chiefly used by lovers, who, seated on the benches with their arms round each other's necks and waists, hugged and caressed each other after the fashion of primeval man, before the public eye.

Such was the town—bleak, black, and desolate, a hive of eating- and of sleeping-boxes, brick-built and roofed with slates.

A dog-fight or a pigeon-flying match, a game of football or of knur and spell, a rabbit-coursing where the whippets tore the rabbits limb from limb, to the delight of all the crowd, more democratic in their love of blood than are their betters at a pheasant battue, were the amusements of the men.

The women stayed at home, working or gossiping across the low stone walls, and fed their children, of whom they had not quivers but whole arsenals well stocked, on Swiss canned milk, tinned meats, and biscuits, to save cookery—an art in which they were so little skilled that what they wasted would have kept two families in any other land.

Upon the Sabbath day they went to chapel, listening to

sermons about hell, of which they heard so much that most of them could have drawn plans of it as accurate as Ordnance Surveys, done with such spirit and regard to truth that the proprietor of the domain might have been proud to hang them in his house.

A sordid class distinction, scarcely apparent at first sight, but yet intense, kept the sport-loving colliers and their employers separate; but yet bound to each other, as marriage binds together man and wife, for the protection of their children's property.

The poisonous air had blasted all the trees, which stood black, gaunt, and sere, leafless and lifeless as they had been the ghosts of forests long departed, in the times when fields were green and England merry, and when the sun shone clear without a pall of intervening smoke.

They stood like finger-posts upon the path to progress, pointing the way, but having perished on the road.

The only highway led into country as desolate as are the mountains of the moon. The gritty hay and oats, which ripened late, fought with the north-east wind, and struggled through the coal-dust in the search for sun, which shone but rarely and as if it were ashamed. Commerce and agriculture seemed to have been about to kiss and then had separated, having drawn back disgusted at each other's countenances.

In the drear fields sheep black as tapirs fed. Their wool could only have been used to make the broadcloth used at funerals. They seemed to feed on refuse, for all the fields were strewn with tins, old boots, and bottles, through which the blighted-looking grass vainly essayed to grow.

But though the aspect of the place was dull and cheerless, almost beyond the wont of northern villages, a silence brooded over it that crept into the soul.

The flag upon the pumping-engine of a new pit close to the railway station was fluttering in the air, showing that coal had recently been struck, but the great wheel was still; no clank of chains marked the descending cage, and on the elevated platform ran no train of trucks to be mechanically tipped over on the bing.

It was not "t' idle day," for generally when colliers "play" the "rows" resound to shouts, the dogs tug at their chains, and streams of men pass in and out the public houses, smoking and talking, if not merrily, at least with that loud Saxon jollity which finds delight in noise.

In the drear town the blinds were all drawn down. Police and soldiers stood about the corners of the streets, and children played in a subdued and melancholy way at reading "T' Riot Act."

Men with their faces scarred with the blue marks that "burning" in the pit imprints on many of their class, lounged, dressed in black, in knots, and talked as dogs might talk after a beating or as slaves when ordered out to death. Their eyes were downcast, and they seemed afraid of something which they could not see, but felt, as children feel the horror of the darkness in a room. Yet through their fears and feeling of amazement mixed with awe, resentment pierced, suppressed but bitter, such as perhaps a horse feels towards his rider who, in his terror at a stumble on a stone, tugs at the bit and violently spurs.

"Government didn't oughter shoot men daawn like that," a scarred old miner muttered, and the rest, the silence broken, soon took up the tale. "Lads didn't rightly knaow what was afoot, when magistrate he come riding oop with t' soldiers and police, and started twittering something out, for all the world like chaffinch; said it was T' Riot Act, and then they fired and shot lad, that's t' bury oop at Oddfellows."

Then by degrees black-coated mourners, dressed in their Sunday clothes, some with the scarves of their society, for "t' corpse" had been "a brother," lounged into the street.

The children stopped their play, and at the gates of the mean houses hosts of women stood, each with a bit of black pinned on their sleeve and faces newly washed. Processions from the neighbouring villages slowly tramped up, and formed before the lodge.

The soldiers and police stared silently, and by degrees the crowd swelled imperceptibly till all the street was full.

Into the lodge the leading "brethren" streamed and seated stiffly, smoked, and in silence spat upon the floor. Their Sunday clothes gave off a smell of camphor, which, mixed with sweat and with the dubbin of their boots, pierced through the fumes of shag and negro-head. Nothing was said for a considerable time, whilst from the crowd outside a murmur rose—as from the cattle in a pen waiting for shipment, as the drovers twist their tails—half pitiful and half resentful; and as the "brethren" heard it, sitting in the smoke, a growl went round, and a man ventured a remark that "Lads could wreck the Riding if they had a mind."

No one responding, he gazed up at the roof and then spat noisily, puffed at his pipe, and swore beneath his breath, whilst his companions pretended that they had not heard, and smoked on silently.

A brother rising stiffly to his feet looked round the room, and after smoothing down his hair, hawked, cleared his throat, and putting his still burning pipe into his waistcoat pocket, called for volunteers to carry "the diseased oop to t' cemetery." When marshals had been duly chosen, not without wrangling, the crowd assembled in the street in which the man "shot by t' Government" had lived. The blinds were all drawn down, but at the gate of all the rows the people stood, and in the misty air the sound of bands converging from the collieries was heard. An ancient hearse drew up before the door, drawn by a chestnut horse, and as they stood and smoked expectant, their hats upon their heads and their black clothes hampering their limbs like fetters, the "brethren," looking at the horse, winked and remarked upon his four white feet, and then recalled the saying that in his case it were best "to return whoam withoot un', for he would never stan' no work."

When the last band had snorted through the street, and not an inch of standing-room was left, "the corpse's brother" went about with wine, followed by several of the dead man's children carrying cake on a Britannia metal dish.

Good manners plainly pointed out to all that they must first refuse, and then on being pressed yield, and break off a bit of cake and ask for "just a bit tastie o' t' wine." Then, on more pressing, resolutely take a good thick slab, and drain the goblet to the bottom till the feast was done, but all in silence and solemnity as the occasion called for, and as the eyes of all the lookers-on demanded should be done. Once more the hawking, red-faced miner stood to the front, and taking off his hat, asked that the minister should pray a bit. Standing upon a chair, the reverend lifted up his voice. Skating upon thin ice, he spoke of the "diseased," praised him and prayed for him, but warily, not wishing to offend the powers that be, but yet indignant at the manner of his death. Then as a melancholy sun shone out and fell on his thin hair, which hung upon the collar of his coat and gave him the appearance of a saint at second hand, he warmed, and launching forth, called on his God to pity and to save, and to provide for "these his children," and he pointed to two girls dressed shabbily in black, who, with a woman holding fast their hands, had been the family of our departed brother in the Lord.

Amens and muttered oaths gurgled up from the crowd, who shuffled with their feet, raising a black and penetrating dust.

The "bit o' prayer" despatched, the minister called for an 'ymn, leading it off himself in such a key that few could compass it. Still they all joined, and as the doggerel floated in the air, raised and prolonged by the rough voices, silently the police took off their helmets under pretence of mopping up their hair. The soldiers listened woodenly, and in the hearse the chestnut horse stamped heavily at flies.

The maimed rites over, the procession got in line, the driver of the hearse seated upon it sideways so as to be in touch with those who followed, and smoking as he drove. In the dark sunless air the tramping feet raised clouds of coal dust, and as men walked they coughed and spat upon the ground, talking in undertones on politics, religion, and the price of coal.

Arrived before "t' cemetery" gate, the hearse drew up; and four tall brothers, taking out the "chest," bore it upon their shoulders to the grave. Four others lowered it, and the Levite, stepping forth, again took up his parable, speaking about the virtues of the dead, of faith, good works, and of the state of man, flowering today, tomorrow failing, and then cast out into the oven—a phrase which, though it might have terrified some men, was taken by his hearers as liturgic and received with groans.

Then he committed to the earth the dead man's body, certain, as he averred, both of the resurrection and the life to come, and on the coffin fell the gritty soil, as if it mocked him by its blackness and its uncompromising grime.

Last act of all, the grave was trodden in, the wooden shoes of those who dug it trampling it hard, as they walked to and fro upon the grass.

All was now over, and the brethren solemnly shook hands, the bands struck up a march, and through the fields the miners straggled homeward, not in procession but confusedly.

Beside the grave two or three mourners smoked a sympathising pipe, and by the hedge the chestnut hearse-horse, with the reins twisted round his feet, nibbled the growing grass, whilst in the fields the purblind pit ponies, the only real gainers by the strike, wandered listlessly about, as if they missed the whirring of the wheels and the familiar gloom.

Beattock for Moffat

The bustle on the Euston platform stopped for an instant to let the men who carried him to the third class compartment pass along the train. Gaunt and emaciated, he looked just at death's door, and, as they propped him in the carriage between two pillows, he faintly said, "Jock, do ye thing I'll live as far as Moffat? I should na' like to die in London in the smoke."

His cockney wife, drying her tears with a cheap hemstitched pocket handkerchief, her scanty town-bred hair looking like wisps of tow beneath her hat, bought from some window in which each individual article was marked at seven-and-sixpence, could only sob. His brother, with the country sun and wind burn still upon his face, and his huge hands hanging like hams in front of him, made answer.

"Andra," he said, "gin ye last as far as Beattock, we'll gie ye a braw hurl back to the farm, syne the bask air, ye ken, and the milk, and, and—but can ye last as far as Beattock, Andra?"

The sick man, sitting with the cold sweat upon his face, his shrunken limbs looking like sticks inside his ill-made

147

black slop suit, after considering the proposition on its merits, looked up, and said, "I should na' like to bet I feel fair boss, God knows; but there, the mischief of it is, he will na' tell ye, so that, as ye may say, his knowlidge has na commercial value. I ken I look as gash as Garscadden. Ye mind, Jock, in the braw auld times, when the auld laird just slipped awa', whiles they were birlin' at the clairet. A braw death, Jock . . . do ye think it'll be rainin' aboot Ecclefechan? Aye . . . sure to be rainin' aboot Lockerbie. Nae Christians there, Jock, a' Johnstones and Jardines, ye mind?"

The wife, who had been occupied with an air cushion, and, having lost the bellows, had been blowing into it till her cheeks seemed almost bursting, and her false teeth were loosened in her head, left off her toil to ask her husband "If 'e could pick a bit of something, a porkpie, or a nice sausage roll, or something tasty," which she could fetch from the refreshment room. The invalid having declined to eat, and his brother having drawn from his pocket a dirty bag, in which were peppermints, gave him a "drop," telling him that he "minded he aye used to like them weel, when the meenister had fairly got into his prelection in the auld kirk, outby."

The train slid almost imperceptibly away, the passengers upon the platform looking after it with that half foolish, half astonished look with which men watch a disappearing train. Then a few sandwich papers rose with the dust almost to the level of the platform, sank again, the clock struck twelve, and the station fell into a half quiescence, like a volcano in the interval between the lava showers. Inside the third class carriage all was quiet until the lights of Harrow shone upon the left, when the sick man, turning himself with difficulty, said, "Good-bye, Harrow-on-the-Hill. I aye liked Harrow for the hill's sake, tho' ye can scarcely ca' yon wee bit mound a hill, Jean."

His wife, who, even in her grief, still smarted under the Scotch variant of her name, which all her life she had pronounced as "Jayne," and who, true cockney as she was, bounded her world within the lines of Plaistow, Peckham Rye, the Welch 'Arp ('Endon way), and Willesden, moved uncomfortably at the depreciation of the chief mountain in her cosmos, but held her peace. Loving her husband in a sort of half antagonistic fashion, born of the difference of type between the hard, unyielding, yet humorous and sentimental Lowland Scot, and the conglomorate of all races of the island which meet in London, and produce the weedy, shallow breed, almost incapable of reproduction, and yet high strung and nervous, there had arisen between them that intangible veil of misconception which, though not excluding love, is yet impervious to respect. Each saw the other's failings, or, perhaps, thought the good qualities which each possessed were faults, for usually men judge each other by their good points, which, seen through prejudice of race, religion, and surroundings, appear to them defects.

The brother, who but a week ago had left his farm unwillingly, just when the "neeps were wantin' heughin' and a feck o' things requirin' to be done, forby a puckle sheep waitin' for keelin'," to come and see his brother for the last time, sat in that dour and seeming apathetic attitude which falls upon the country man, torn from his daily toil, and plunged into a town. Most things in London, during the brief intervals he had passed away from the sick bed, seemed foolish to him, and of a nature such as a self-respecting Moffat man, in the hebdomadal enjoyment of the "prelections" of a Free Church minister could not authorise.

"Man, saw ye e'er a carter sittin' on his cart, and drivin' at a trot, instead o' walkin' in a proper manner alangside his horse?" had been his first remark.

The short-tailed sheep dogs, and the way they worked, the inferior quality of the cart horses, their shoes with hardly any calkins worth the name, all was repugnant to him.

On Sabbath, too, he had received a shock, for, after walking miles to sit under the "brither of the U.P. minister at Symington," he had found Erastian hymn books in the pews, and noticed with stern reprobation that the congregation stood to sing, and that, instead of sitting solidly whilst the "man wrastled in prayer," stooped forward in the fashion called the Nonconformist lounge.

His troubled spirit had received refreshment from the sermon, which, though short, and extending to but some five-and-forty minutes, had still been powerful, for he said:

"When yon wee, shilpit meenister—brither, ye ken, of rantin' Ferguson, out by Symington—shook the congregation ower the pit mouth, ye could hae fancied that the very sowls in hell just girned. Man, he garred the very stour to flee aboot the kirk, and, hadna' the big book been weel brass banded, he would hae dang the haricles fair oot."

So the train slipped past Watford, swaying round the curves like a gigantic serpent, and jolting at the facing points as a horse "pecks" in his gallop at an obstruction in the ground.

The moon shone brightly into the compartment, extinguishing the flickering of the half candlepower electric light. Rugby, the station all lit up, and with its platforms occupied but by a few belated passengers, all muffled up like race horses taking their exercise, flashed past. They slipped through Cannock Chase, which stretches down with heath and firs, clear brawling streams, and birch trees, an outpost of the north lost in the midland clay. They crossed the oily Trent, flowing through alder copses, and with its backwaters all overgrown with lilies, like an *aguape* in Paraguay or in Brazil.

The sick man, wrapped in cheap rugs, and sitting like Guy Fawkes, in the half comic, half pathetic way that sick folk sit, making them sport for fools, and, at the same time, moistening the eye of the judicious, who reflect that they themselves may one day sit as they do, bereft of all the dignity of strength, looked listlessly at nothing as the train sped on. His loving, tactless wife, whose cheap "sized" handkerchief had long since become a rag with mopping up her tears, endeavoured to bring round her husband's thoughts to paradise, which she conceived a sort of music hall, where angels sat with their wings folded, listening to sentimental songs.

Her brother-in-law, reared on the fiery faith of Moffat Calvinism, eyed her with great disfavour, as a terrier eyes a rat imprisoned in a cage.

"Jean wumman," he burst out, "to hear ye talk, I would jist think your meenister had been a perfectly illeeterate man, pairadise here, pairadise there, what do ye think a man like Andra could dae daunderin' about a gairden naked, pu'in soor aipples frae the trees?"

Cockney and Scotch conceit, impervious alike to outside criticism, and each so bolstered in its pride as to be quite incapable of seeing that anything existed outside the purlieus of their sight, would soon have made the carriage into a battle-field, had not the husband, with the authority of approaching death, put in his word.

"Whist, Jeanie wumman. Jock, dae ye no ken that the Odium-Theologicum is just a curse—pairadise—set ye baith up—pairadise. I dinna' even richtly ken if I can last as far as Beattock."

Stafford, its iron furnaces belching out flames, which burned red holes into the night, seemed to approach, rather than be approached, so smoothly ran the train. The mingled moonlight and the glare of iron-works lit the canal beside the railway, and from the water rose white

vapours as from Styx or Periphlegethon. Through Chesh-
ire ran the train, its timbered houses showing ghastly in
the frost which coated all the carriage windows, and rendered them opaque. Preston, the catholic city, lay silent in
the night, its river babbling through the public park, and
then the hills of Lancashire loomed lofty in the night. Past
Garstang, with its water-lily-covered ponds, Garstang
where, in the days gone by, catholic squires, against their
will, were forced on Sundays to "take wine" in Church on
pain of fine, the puffing serpent slid.

The talk inside the carriage had given place to sleep,
that is, the brother-in-law and wife slept fitfully, but the
sick man looked out, counting the miles to Moffat, and
speculating on his strength. Big drops of sweat stood on
his forehead, and his breath came double, whistling
through his lungs.

They passed by Lancaster, skirting the sea on which the
moon shone bright, setting the fishing boats in silver as
they lay scarcely moving on the waves. Then, so to speak,
the train set its face up against Shap Fell, and, puffing
heavily, drew up into the hills, the scattered grey stone
houses of the north, flanked by their gnarled and twisted
ash trees, hanging upon the edge of the streams, as lonely,
and as cut off from the world (except the passing train) as
they had been in Central Africa. The moorland roads,
winding amongst the heather, showed that the feet of
generations had marked them out, and not the line, spade,
and theodolite, with all the circumstance of modern road
makers. They, too, looked white and unearthly in the
moonlight, and now and then a sheep, aroused by the
snorting of the train, moved from the heather into the
middle of the road, and stood there motionless, its shadow
filling the narrow track, and flickering on the heather at
the edge.

The keen and penetrating air of the hills and night

roused the two sleepers, and they began to talk, after the Scottish fashion, of the funeral, before the anticipated corpse.

"Ye ken, we've got a braw new hearse outby, sort of Epescopalian lookin', wi' gless a' roond, so's ye can see the kist. Very conceity too, they mak' the hearses noo-a-days. I min' when they were jist auld sort o' ruckly boxes, awfu' licht, ye ken upon the springs, and just went dodderin' alang, the body swinging to and fro, as if it would flee richt oot. The roads, ye ken, were no nigh hand so richtly metalled in thae days."

The subject of the conversation took it cheerfully, expressing pleasure at the advance of progress as typified in the new hearse, hoping his brother had a decent "stan' o' black," and looking at his death, after the fashion of his kind, as it were something outside himself, a fact indeed, on which, at the same time, he could express himself with confidence as being in some measure interested. His wife, not being Scotch, took quite another view, and seemed to think that the mere mention of the word was impious, or, at the least, of such a nature as to bring on immediate dissolution, holding the English theory that unpleasant things should not be mentioned, and that, by this means, they can be kept at bay. Half from affection, half from the inborn love of cant, inseparable from the true Anglo-Saxon, she endeavoured to persuade her husband that he looked better, and yet would mend, once in his native air.

"At Moffit, ye'd 'ave the benefit of the 'ill breezes, and that 'ere country milk, which never 'as no cream in it, but 'olesome, as you say. Why yuss, in about eight days at Moffit, you'll be as 'earty as you ever was. Yuss, you will, you take my word."

Like a true Londoner, she did not talk religion, being too thin in mind and body even to have grasped the dogma of any of the sects. Her Heaven a music 'all, her paradise to see the king drive through the streets, her literary pleasure to read lies in newspapers, or pore on novelettes, which showed her the pure elevated lives of duchesses, placing the knaves and prostitutes within the limits of her own class; which view of life she accepted as quite natural, and as a thing ordained to be by the bright stars who write.

Just at the Summit they stopped an instant to let a goods train pass, and, in a faint voice, the consumptive said, "I'd almost lay a wager now I'd last to Moffat, Jock. The Shap, ye ken, I aye looked at as the beginning of the run home. The hills, ye ken, are sort 'o heartsome. No that they're bonny hills like Moffat hills, na', na', ill-shapen sort of things, just like Borunty tatties, awfu' puir names too, Shap Fell and Rowland Edge, Hutton Roof Crags, and Arnside Fell; heard ever ony body sich like names for hills? Naething to fill the mooth; man, the Scotch hills jist grap ye in the mooth for a' the world like speerits."

They stopped at Penrith, which the old castle walls make even meaner, in the cold morning light, than other stations look. Little Salkeld, and Armathwaite, Cotehill, and Scotby all rushed past, and the train, slackening, stopped with a jerk upon the platform, at Carlisle. The sleepy porters bawled out "change for Maryport," some drovers slouched into carriages, kicking their dogs before them, and, slamming to the doors, exchanged the time of day with others of their tribe, all carrying ash or hazel sticks, all red faced and keen eyed, their caps all crumpled, and their great-coat tails all creased, as if their wearers had laid down to sleep full dressed, so as to lose no time in getting to the labours of the day. The old red sandstone church, with something of a castle in its look, as well befits a shrine close to a frontier where in days gone by the priest had need to watch and pray, frowned on the passing train, and on the manufactories, whose banked up fires sent poisonous fumes into the air, withering the trees which, in the public park, a careful council had hedged round about with wire.

The Eden ran from bank to bank, its water swirling past as wildly as when "The Bauld Buccleugh" and his Moss Troopers, bearing "the Kinmount" fettered in their midst, plunged in and passed it, whilst the keen Lord Scroope stood on the brink amazed and motionless. Gretna, so close to England, and yet a thousand miles away in speech and feeling, found the sands now flying through the glass. All through the mosses which once were the "Debateable Land" on which the moss-troopers of the clan Graeme were used to hide the cattle stolen from the "auncient enemy," the now repatriated Scotchman murmured feebly "that it was bonny scenery" although a drearier prospect of "moss hags" and stunted birch trees is not to be found. At Ecclefechan he just raised his head, and faintly spoke of "yon auld carl, Carlyle, ye ken, a dour thrawn body, but a gran' pheelosopher," and then lapsed into silence, broken by frequent struggles to take breath.

His wife and brother sat still, and eyed him as a cow watches a locomotive engine pass, amazed and helpless, and he himself had but the strength to whisper "Jock, I'm dune, I'll no' see Moffat, blast it, yon smoke, ye ken, yon London smoke has been ower muckle for ma lungs."

The tearful, helpless wife, not able even to pump up the harmful and unnecessary conventional lie, which after all, consoles only the liar, sat pale and limp, chewing the fingers of her Berlin gloves. Upon the weather-beaten cheek of Jock glistened a tear, which he brushed off as angrily as it had been a wasp.

"Aye, Andra'," he said, "I would hae liket awfu' weel that ye should win to Moffat. Man, the rowan trees are a' in bloom, and there's a bonny breer upon the corn—aye, ou aye, the reid bogs are lookin' gran' the year—but Andra', I'll tak' ye east to the auld kirk yaird, ye'll no' ken onything aboot it, but we'll hae a heartsome funeral."

Lockerbie seemed to fly towards them, and the dying Andra' smiled as his brother pointed out the place and said, "Ye mind, there are no ony Christians in it," and answered, "Aye, I mind, naething but Jardines," as he fought for breath.

The death dews gathered on his forehead as the train shot by Nethercleugh, passed Wamphray, and Dinwoodie, and with a jerk pulled up at Beattock just at the summit of the pass.

So in the cold spring morning light, the fine rain beating on the platform, as the wife and brother got their almost speechless care out of the carriage, the brother whispered, "Dam't, ye've done it, Andra', here's Beattock; I'll tak' ye east to Moffat yet to dee."

But on the platform, huddled on the bench to which he had been brought, Andra' sat speechless and dying in the rain. The doors banged to, the guard stepping in lightly as the train flew past, and a belated porter shouted, "Beattock, Beattock for Moffat," and then, summoning his last strength, Andra' smiled, and whispered faintly in his brother's ear, "Aye, Beattock—for Moffat?" Then his head fell back, and a faint bloody foam oozed from his pallid lips. His wife stood crying helplessly, the rain beating upon the flowers of her cheap hat, rendering it shapeless and ridiculous. But Jock, drawing out a bottle, took a short dram and saying, "Andra', man, ye made a richt gude fecht o' it," snorted an instant in a red pocket handkerchief, and calling up a boy, said, "Rin, Jamie, to the toon, and tell McNicol to send up and fetch a corp." Then, after helping to remove the body to the waiting room, walked out into the rain, and, whistling "Corn Rigs" quietly between his teeth lit up his pipe, and muttered as he smoked "A richt gude fecht—man aye, ou aye, a game yin Andra', puir felly. Weel, weel, he'll hae a braw hurl onyway in the new Moffat hearse."

Might, Majesty and Dominion

A nation dressed in black, a city wreathed in purple hangings, woe upon every face, and grief in every heart. A troop of horses in the streets ridden by kings; a fleet of ships from every nation upon earth; all the world's business stilled for three long days to mourn the passing of her who was the mother of her people, even of the poorest of her people in the land. The newspapers all diapered in black, the clouds dark grey and sullen, and a hush upon the islands, and upon all their vast dependencies throughout the world. Not only for the passing of the Queen, the virtuous woman, the good mother, the slave of duty; but because she was the mother of her people, even the poorest of her people in the land. Sixty odd years of full prosperity; England advancing towards universal Empire; an advance in the material arts of progress such as the world has never known; and yet to-day she who was to most Englishmen the concentration of the national idea, borne on a gun-carriage through the same streets which she had so often passed through in the full joy of life. Full sixty years of progress; wages at least thrice higher than, when a girl, she mounted on her throne; England's dominions

157

more than thrice extended; arts, sciences, and everything that tends to bridge space over, a thousand times advanced, and a new era brought about by steam and electricity, all in the lifetime of her who passed so silently through the once well-known streets. The national wealth swollen beyond even the dreams of those who saw the beginning of the reign; churches innumerable built by the pious care of those who thought the gospel should be brought home to the poor. Great battleships, torpedo boats, submarine vessels, guns, rifles, stinkpot shells, and all the contrivances of those who think that the material progress of the Anglo-Saxon race should enter into the polity of savage states, as Latin used to enter schoolboys' minds, with blood. Again, a hum of factories in the land, wheels whizzing, bands revolving so rapidly that the eye of man can hardly follow them, making machinery a tangled mass of steel, heaving and jumping in its action, so that the unpractical looker-on fears that some bolt may break and straight destroy him, like a cannon ball.

All this, and coal mines, with blast furnaces, and smelting works with men half-naked working by day and night before the fires. Infinite and incredible contrivances to save all labour; aerial ships projected; speech practicable between continents without the aid of wires; charities such as the world has never known before; a very cacoethes of good doing; a sort of half-baked goodwill to all men, so that the charities came from superfluous wealth and the goodwill is of platonic kind; all this and more during the brief dream of sixty years in which the ruler, she who was mother of her people, trod the earth. All these material instances of the great change in human life, which in her reign had happened, and which she suffered unresistingly, just as the meanest of her subjects suffered them, and as both she and they welcomed the sun from heaven as something quite outside of them, and, as it were, ordained, her people, in some dull faithful way, had grown into the habit of connecting in some vague manner with herself. For sixty years, before the most of us now living had uttered our first cry, she held the orb and sceptre, and appeared to us a mother Atlas, to sustain the world. She left us, almost without a warning, and a nation mourned her, because she was the mother of her people, yes, even of the meanest of her people in the land.

So down the streets in the hard biting wind, right through the rows of dreary living-boxes which like a tunnel seemed to encase the assembled mass of men, her funeral procession passed. On housetops and on balconies her former subjects swarmed like bees; the trees held rookeries of men, and the keen wind swayed them about, but still they kept their place, chilled to the bone but uncomplainingly, knowing their former ruler had been the mother of them all.

Emperors and kings passed on, the martial pomp and majesty of glorious war clattering and clanking at their heels. The silent crowds stood reverently all dressed in black. At length, when the last soldier had ridden out of sight, the torrent of humanity broke into myriad waves, leaving upon the grass of the down-trodden park its scum of sandwich papers, which, like the foam of some great ocean, clung to the railings, round the roots of trees, was driven fitfully before the wind over the boot-stained grass, or trodden deep into the mud, or else swayed rhythmically to and fro as seaweed sways and moans in the slack water of a beach.

At length they all dispersed, and a well-bred and well-fed dog or two roamed to and fro, sniffing disdainfully at the remains of the rejected food which the fallen papers held.

Lastly, a man grown old in the long reign of the much-mourned ruler whose funeral procession had just passed, stumbled about, slipping upon the muddy grass, and taking up a paper from the mud fed ravenously on that which the two dogs had looked at with disdain.

His hunger satisfied, he took up of the fragments that remained a pocketful, and then, whistling a snatch from a forgotten opera, slouched slowly onward and was swallowed by the gloom.

An Idealist

The comrade who had lectured having sat down amidst
applause, the chairman asked for questions on the speech.
In the long narrow hall the audience sat like sardines in a
box, so thickly packed that they had hardly room to shout.
The greater part were workmen, but workmen of the
London type, sallow and slight and dressed in cheap slop
clothes. Some foreigners gave colour to the gathering, and
showed up curiously against a sprinkling of middle-class
inquirers after truth. The latter, mostly, were callow-
looking, earnest young men from various provincial universities, dressed in grey flannel suits with green or yellow
neckties, their fluffy hair looking as if it never had been
brushed, and their long scraggy throats so thin, one wondered they contained the enormous Adam's apple which
protruded over the low-cut collar of their shirts. One or
two ladies, chiefly dressed in stuffs from Liberty's, sat
half-constrainedly, and jotted down either impressions of
the scene or notes of the more salient portions of the
lecturer's remarks. Three or four comrades, of the kind
whose daily life is Socialism, that is of course talking about
it, and laying off what the world will be like at its glad

advent, sat in front places, and now and then during the progress of the lecture had interjected an "'Ear, 'ear" or "Let 'em 'ave it," meaning of course the Bourgeois, who certainly that evening must have trembled in his shoes, to hear his vices publicly unveiled. They had a kind of likeness to the men who in the Quartier Latin remain art-students all their lives, wearing wide peg-top trousers, flat-brimmed hats, and flapping neckties of black crêpe de Chine, and who in cafés spout continually of art, and in their way are comrades, thinking that everlasting talk is the best way to paint a picture or to revolutionize the world. In front at a deal table sat one or two reporters, dull and uninterested, to whom all creeds and faiths were equal, and any kind of lecture or of speech, so many hours of tedious work, which they, bound to work out their purgatory here on earth, lived by reporting at so much the column or the thousand words.

Over the hall there hung that odour of hot people, and stale scent, mixed with the fumes of coarse tobacco in the clothes, which is the true particular flavour of all meetings, Tory and Socialist alike, just as in times gone by extract of orange peel and sawdust marked a circus, or as in Catholic countries incense tones down the various smells which rise from off the faithful in a church.

No one responding to the chairman's call, he just had risen up to thank "our comrade for his eloquent, well thought out and delivered lecture, which all who 'eard it must allow was miles a'ead of all the frothy utterances of members of the two parties of boss frauds between 'oom laybour 'angs, as 'e might say upon the cross, the Liberals and Tories, 'ypocrites and Pharisees . . . if ever there was 'umbugs . . ." when a man arose and said "Excuse me, Mr. Chayrman, I 'aven't got a question, but seeing you was arsting for one, I'd like to say a word."

Boys seated in the gallery, to whom according to their

philosophic state of boydom all meetings and all speeches simply were chances for diversion, shouted out " 'Ear, 'ear, I saay let Betterton 'ave 'arf a mo'."

The chairman half-constrainedly resumed his seat, baulked like a fiery horse at yeomanry manoeuvres, in full career, and toying with the water-bottle, on which great drops of moisture hung condensed, called upon Comrade Betterton, with a request he would be brief. A little withered-looking man of about seventy stood up, yellow in colour as old parchment, and with some still remaining wisps of yellowish, grey hair hanging about his head, like seaweed on a rock. His clothes were rusty black, and neatly brushed, his faded eyes of porcelain blue, were set in rims of red, his knees were shaky, and his whole being was pervaded by an air of great benevolence. Clearing his throat and looking round the hall with the assurance of a practised speaker, he broke into a breathless sentence, fluent, unpunctuated, and evidently well known to the admiring boys, who cheered him to the fray.

"I've 'eard the speech," he said, "of the comrade who has addressed us at some length, I've heard and think it 'umbug. As Shakespeare says, whilst the grass grows, the 'orse is starving." At this quotation a boy yelled "Why the 'ell don't he eat it then?" The ladies coloured, fearing the social revolution had actually begun, and from the chairman came the hope that the audience would keep to parliamentary language "seein' that there was lydies in the 'all." Then having called upon our comrade to resume and not to take up too much time, and order being once again established, Betterton took up his interrupted speech, just as a phonograph, cut off, begins again exactly at the place where it was stopped. "What do I find? Nothing but all the means of livelihood monopolize, means of production in the 'ands of one set, land in the other, even the raw material all taken up by the capitalists. Things I say, comrades, is gettin' daily worse, nothin' being left on which a man can exercise his lybour, without a tax to pay to somebody for doin' it. What is a man to do? Sometimes I think, all I can do is to go out and throw a bomb of dynamite involvin' in the sayme destruction all the blood-suckin' sweaters and land monopolists alike . . ." What more the speaker might have said, Providence only and the boys seated in the gallery knew, for a voice emanating from the body of the hall was heard to say in a sarcastic tone, "Why don't you go and throw it?" and in the shouts of laughter that ensued, the speaker discomfited, but still benevolent for all his fiery words, subsided in his seat, and with the usual compliments and the collection, without which no meeting, Socialist, Anarchist, Liberal, religious or Conservative, can ever end, the hall was emptied in a trice, the audience passing swiftly, with their eyes fixed on vacancy, before the comrades who at the door sat selling "literatoor."

This was the first occasion that Betterton revealed himself to my unworthy eyes. As time went on I knew him better, and became so to speak one of his intimates, for there are many kinds of intimates, besides the sort you eat and drink with and stand with in the club windows, to criticize the ladies' ankles as they pass. In the first place, he lived on bread and milk, thinking it wrong to take the life of anything (except of course a Bourgeois), so that the pleasures of the table were not exactly in his way.

The work of his profession, that of billsticker, took him far from my haunts, and caused him now and then some qualms of conscience, as when he had to cover hoardings with the announcements of some stuff or other which he knew was made by sweated work. An atheist by choice and by conviction, he yet had texts of Scripture always in his mouth, and used to say, "Only I know you see the laybourer is worthy of his 'ire, or now and then I should just chuck it, it 'urts me to be covering up an 'oarding with a great picture of some 'arlot, for the advertisement of some bloodsucker's soap. An' badly drawn too, bad art" (for he was great on art) "and sweated stuff, not that I've anything to say against a 'arlot in herself, the most of them is driven to it by the rich."

As to why this should be, or how, he did not condescend to explanation, but still believed it firmly, holding as the chief axiom of his faith the wickedness of peers, who he apparently considered had as much power, for evil, as the French aristocracy before the Revolution, or as Beelzebub. But notwithstanding poverty and the whole hive of bees he carried in his bonnet, his life was happy and his faith so great it might have moved the House of Commons from its foundations in the mud, could he have found a lever ready to his hand. As it was, at his lodgings in a slum in Drury Lane, he used to issue broad-sheets, printed and set up by himself, on yellow packing paper. The one on which he prided himself most was headed *Messalina,* under which style and title he typified the Queen.

"Pause, brutal and licentious old queen," it opened, "and think, if you have time to think, in the wild orgies of your bestial career." It finished with an adjuration to the pro-letariat to unite, and the last line was "Blood, Blood, Blood, Heads off, Freedom and Liberty for all."

No larger than a sheet of notepaper, the little periodical was stuffed, so he averred, as full of facts as an egg is with meat, and naturally was never paid for, but placed by him upon his daily round in letter-boxes of houses of the rich. One of his pleasures (and they were few and innocent enough) was to depict the feelings of the lord into whose letter-box he had deposited his squib. "When he sits after dinner, drinking his port wine, with his boots off before the fire, it will go through him like a small-tooth comb, and maybe mayke 'im tremble, perhaps touch up his 'eart—

who knows?—sometimes those kind of chaps is not all bad, only they eats and drinks too much, and 'as no time to think."

Not a dull day could Comrade Betterton remember in his whole life.

"Talk of the Greeks and Romans," he used to say, "of course the Romans mostly was bourgwaw, like ourselves, but the Greeks certainly 'ad opportunities. I mean in art and such-like, and seeing people go about without their clothes, thus gettin' rid of all 'ypocrisy and that, but then as to an ideal for hewmanity, they was deficient. All art was for a class. Now we live in a glorious time, I wouldn't 'a missed it for a lot. But, as to art, exceptin' poor old Morris, most o' your painters and litteratoors and such is middle-class in their ideas, thinks that their kind of stuff is only for the cultivated classes, . . . and see your cultivated class, always at races and shootin' pheasants, . . . care as much about the arts as dockers down in Canning Town. What I mean is, a man like me 'as 'is ideal nowadays, and can look forward to a time, when all them Bastilles is pulled down, . . . it's figuratively I use the word. You needn't larf. . . . It does a man's 'eart good to look forward to a time when all your middle-class ideals shall be swept away, and mankind let alone, to grow up beautiful, 'ealthy, artistic, and as unmoral as the Greeks. That 'ere morality has been the curse of men of my class, making 'em 'ypocrites and driving 'em to drink."

So he went on bill-sticking for his daily bread and moralising always, both in and out of season, and testifying to his faith with all the unction of a martyr at the stake; as once, when at a public meeting packed to the ceiling with religious folk, someone averred he spoke, as he hoped, "in the spirit of my master, Christ," Betterton, rising from his seat, remarked, " 'E ain't my master, Sir."

Benevolent and yet ridiculous, kindly, half mad, and

shrewd in all his speculations upon life, on things, on motives, and on men, most likely years ago his bills are covered over an inch thick with others, his pot of paste turned mouldy, his brushes worn down to the wood, and he himself safely enfeoffed in the possession of the inheritance to which he had been born, a pauper's funeral, and grave.

Still, when I sometimes look on his life's work in literature, the pamphlet *Messalina,* in which poor Queen Victoria is both so roundly and unjustly vilified, and think upon the pleasure that no doubt the writer had in its production in his one stuffy room in Drury Lane, it is not always easy to be sure, if one should laugh or cry.

Christie Christison

Of all the guests that used to come to Claraz's Hotel, there was none stranger or more interesting than Christie Christison, a weatherbeaten sailor who still spoke his native dialect of Peterhead despite his thirty years out in the Plate. He used to bring an air into the room with him of old salt fish and rum, and of cold wintry nights in the low latitudes down by the Horn. This, too, though it was years since he had been at sea.

Although the world had gone so well with him, and by degrees he had become one of the biggest merchants in the place, he yet preserved the speech and manners of a Greenland whaler, which calling he had followed in his youth.

The Arctic cold and tropic suns during the years that he had traded up and down the coast had turned his naturally fair complexion to a mottled hue, and whisky, or the sun, had touched his nose so fiercely that it furnished a great fund of witticism amongst the other guests.

Mansel said that the skipper's nose reminded him of the port light of an old sugar droger, and Cossart had it, that no chemist's window in Montmartre had any *flacon*, bottle you call him, eh? of such resplendent hue. Most of them knew he had a history, but no one ever heard him tell it, although it was well known he had come out from Peterhead in the dark ages, when Rosas terrorised the Plate, in his own schooner, the *Rosebud,* and piled her up at last, somewhere on the Patagonian coast, upon a trip down to the Falkland Islands. He used to talk about his schooner as if she had been one of the finest craft afloat; but an old Yankee skipper, who had known her, swore she was a bull-nosed, round-sterned sort of oyster-mouching vessel, with an old deck-house like a town hall, straight-sided, and with a lime-juice look about her that made him tired.

Whatever were her merits or her faults, she certainly had made her skipper's fortune, or at least laid the foundation of it; for, having started as a trader, he gradually began to act half as a carrier, half as a mail-boat, going to Stanley every three months or so with mails and letters, and coming back with wool.

Little by little, aided by his wife, a stout, hard-featured woman from his native town, he got a little capital into his hands.

When he was on a voyage, Jean used to search about to get a cargo for his next trip, so that when the inevitable came and the old *Rosebud* ran upon the reef down at San Julian, Christie was what he called "weel-daein," and forsook the sea for good.

He settled down in Buenos Aires as a woolbroker, and by degrees altered his clothes to the full-skirted coat of Melton cloth with ample side-pockets, the heather-mixture trousers, and tall white hat, with a black band, that formed his uniform up to his dying day. He wore a Newgate frill of beard, and a blue necktie, which made a striking contrast with his face, browned by the sun and wind, and skin like a dried piece of mare's hide, through which the colour of his northern blood shone darkly, like the red in an old-fashioned cooking apple after a touch of frost.

Except a few objurgatory phrases, he had learned no

Spanish, and his own speech remained the purest dialect of Aberdeenshire—coarse, rough and racy, and double-shotted with an infinity of oaths, relics of his old whaling days, when as he used to say he started life, like a young rook, up in the crow's-nest of a bluff-bowed and broad-beamed five-hundred barrel boat, sailing from Peterhead.

Things had gone well with him, and he had taken to himself as partner a fellow-countryman, one Andrew Nicolson, who had passed all his youth in Edinburgh, in an insurance office. Quiet, unassuming, and yet not without traces of that pawky humour which few Scots are born entirely lacking in, he had fallen by degrees into a sort of worship of his chief, whose sallies, rough and indecent as they often were, fairly convulsed him, making him laugh until the tears ran down his face, as he exclaimed, "Hear to him, man, he's awfu' rich, I'm tellin' ye."

Christie took little notice of his adoration except to say, "Andra man, dinna expose yourself," or something of the kind.

In fact, no one could understand how two such ill-assorted men came to be friends, except perhaps because they both were Scotchmen, or because Andrew's superior education and well-brushed black clothes appealed to Christison.

He himself could not write, but knew enough to sign his name, which feat he executed with many puffings, blowings, and an occasional oath.

Still he was shrewd in business, which he executed almost entirely by telegram, refusing to avail himself of any code, saying he "couldna stand them; some day ye lads will get a cargo of dolls' eyes, when ye have sent for maize. Language is gude enough for me, I hae no secrets. Damn yer monkey talk."

His house at Florés was the place of call of all the ship captains who visited the port. There they would sit and drink, talking about the want of lights on such and such a coast, of skippers who had lost their ships twenty or thirty years ago, the price of whale oil, and of things that interest their kind; whilst Mrs. Christison sat knitting, looking as if she never in her life had moved from Peterhead, in her grey gown and woollen shawl, fastened across her breast by a brooch, with a picture of her man, "in natural colouring." Their life was homely, and differed little from what it had been in the old days when they were poor, except that now and then they took the air in an old battered carriage—which Christison had taken for a debt—looking uncomfortable and stiff, dressed in their Sunday clothes. Their want of knowledge of the language of the place kept them apart from others of their class, and Christison, although he swore by Buenos Aires, which he had seen emerge from a provincial town to a great city, yet cursed the people, calling them a "damned set of natives," which term he generally applied to all but Englishmen.

Certainly nothing was more unlike a "native" than the ex-skipper now turned merchant, in his ways, speech, and dress. Courtesy, which was innate in natives of the place, was to him not only quite superfluous, but a thing to be avoided, whilst his strange habit of devouring bread fresh from the oven, washed down with sweet champagne, gained him the name of the "Scotch Ostrich," which nickname he accepted in good part as a just tribute to his digestive powers, remarking that "the Baptist, John, ye mind, aye fed on locusts and wild honey, and a strong man aye liked strong meat, all the worrld o'er."

In the lives of the elderly Aberdeenshire couple, few would have looked for a romantic story, for the hard-featured merchant and his quiet home-keeping wife appeared so happy and contented in their snug villa on the Florés road. No one in Buenos Aires suspected anything, and most likely Christison would have died, remembered only by his tall white hat, had he not one day chosen to tell his tale.

A fierce pampero had sprung up in an hour, the sky had turned that vivid green that marks storms from the south in Buenos Aires. Whirlfire kept the sky lighted, till an arch had formed in the south-east, and then the storm broke, blinding and terrible, with a strange, seething noise. The wind, tearing along the narrow streets, forced everyone to fly for refuge.

People on foot darted into the nearest house, and horsemen, flying like birds before the storm, sought refuge anywhere they could, their horses, slipping and sliding on the rough, paved streets, sending out showers of sparks as they stopped suddenly, just as a skater sends out a spray of ice. The deep-cut streets, with their raised pavements, soon turned to watercourses, from three to four feet deep, through which the current ran so fiercely that it was quite impossible to pass on foot. The horsemen, galloping for shelter, passed through them with the water banking up against their horses on the stream side, though they plied whip and spurs.

After the first hour of the tempest, when a little light began to dawn towards the south, and the peals of thunder slacken a little in intensity, men's nerves became relaxed from the over-tension that a pampero brings with it, just as if nature had been overwound, and by degrees was paying out the chain.

Storm-stayed at Claraz's sat several men, Cossart, George Mansel, one Don José Hernández and Christie Christison. Perhaps the pampero had strung up his nerves, or perhaps the desire that all men feel at times to tell what is expedient they should keep concealed, impelled him; but at any rate he launched into the story of his life, to the amazement of his friends, who never thought he either had a story to impart, or if he had that it would ever issue from his lips.

"Ye mind the *Rosebud*?" he remarked.

None of the assembled men had ever seen her, although she still was well remembered on the coast.

"Weel, weel, I mind the time she was well kent, a bonny craft. Old Andrew Reid o' Buckieside, he built her, back in the fifties. When he went under, he had to sell his house of Buckieside. I bought her cheap.

"It's fifteen years and mair, come Martinmas, since I piled her up. . . . I canna think how I managed it, knowing the bay, San Julian, ye ken, sae weel.

"It was a wee bit hazy, but still I thought I could get in wi' the blue pigeon going.

"I mind it yet, ye see you hae to keep the rocks where they say they ganakers all congregate before they die, right in a line with yon bit island.

"I heard the water shoaling as the leadsman sung out in the chains, but still kept on, feeling quite sure I knew the channel, when, bang she touches, grates a little, and sticks dead fast, wi' a long shiver o' her keel. Yon rocks must have been sharp as razors, for she began to fill at once.

"No chance for any help down in San Julian Bay in those days, nothing but ane o' they *pulperías* kept by a Basque, a wee bit place, wi' a ditch and bank, and a small brass cannon stuck above the gate. I got what gear I could into the boat, and started for the beach.

"Jean, myself, three o' the men, and an old Dago I carried with me as an interpreter.

"The other sailormen, and a big dog we had aboard, got into the other boat, and we all came ashore. Luckily it was calm, and the old *Rosebud* had struck not above two or three hundred yards from land. Man, San Julian was a dreich place in they days, naething but the bit fortified *pulpería* I was tellin' ye aboot. The owner, old Don Augusty, a Basque, ye ken, just ca'ed his place the 'Rose of the South.' He micht as well have called it the Rose of Sharon. Deil a rose for miles, or any other sort of flower.

"Well, men, next day it just began to blow, and in a day or two knockit the old *Rosebud* fair to matchwood. Jean, she grat sair to see her gae to bits, and I cursit a while, though I felt like greetin' too, I'm tellin' ye. There we were sort o' marooned, a' the lot of us, without a chance of getting off maybe for months; for in these days devil a ship but an odd whaler now and then ever came nigh the place. By a special mercy Yanquetruz's band of they Pehuelches happened to come to trade.

"Quiet enough folk yon Indians, and Yanquetruz himself had been brocht up in Buenos Aires in a mission school.

"Man, a braw fellow! Six foot six at least, and sat his horse just like a picture. We bought horses from him, and got a man to guide us up to the Welsh settlement at Chubut, a hundred leagues away.

"Richt gude beasts they gave us, and we got through fine, though I almost thocht I had lost Jean.

"Yanquetruz spoke English pretty well, Spanish of course, and as I tellt ye, he was a bonny man.

"Weel, he sort o' fell in love wi' Jean, and one day he came up to the *pulpería*, and getting off his horse, a braw black piebald wi' an eye like fire intil him, he asked to speak to me. First we had Caña, and then Carlón, then some more Caña, and yon *vino seco,* and syne some more Carlón. I couldna richtly see what he was driving at. However, all of a sudden he says, 'Wife very pretty, Indian he like buy.'

"I told him Christians didna sell their wives, and we had some more Caña, and then he says, 'Indian like Christian woman, she more big, more white than Indian girl.'

"To make a long tale short, he offered me his horse and fifty dollars, then several ganaker skins, they ca' them *guillapices,* and finally in addition a mare and foal. Man, they were bonny beasts, both red roan piebalds, and to pick any Indian girl I liked. Not a bad price down there at San Julian, where the chief could hae cut all our throats had he been minded to.

"... Na, na, we werna' fou, just a wee miraculous. Don Augusty was sort o' scared when he heard what Yanquetruz was saying, and got his pistol handy and a bit axe he keepit for emergencies behind the counter. Losh me, yon Yanquetruz was that ceevil, a body couldna tak fuff at him.

"At last I told him I wasna on to trade, and we both had a tot of square-faced gin to clean our mouths a bit, and oot to the *palenque,* where the chief's horse was tied.

"A bonny beastie, his mane hogged and cut into castles, like a clipped yew hedge, his tail plaited and tied with a piece of white mare's hide, and everything upon him solid silver, just like a dinner-service.

"The chief took his spear in his hand—it had been stuck into the ground—and leaning on it, loupit on his horse. Ye ken they deevils mount frae the off-side. He gied a yell that fetched his Indians racing. They had killed a cow, and some of them were daubed with blood; for they folk dinna wait for cooking when they are sharp set. Others were three-parts drunk, and came stottering along, with square-faced gin bottles in their hands.

"Their horses werna tied, nor even hobbled. Na, na, they just stood waiting with the reins upon the ground. Soon as they saw the chief—I canna tell ye how the thing was done—they widna mount, they didna loup, they just melted on their beasts, catching the spears out of the ground as they got up.

"Sirs me, they Indians just took flight like birds, raising sich yellochs, running their horses up against each other, twisting and turning and carrying on in sich a way, just like fishing-boats running for harbour at Buckie or Montrose.

"Our guide turned out a richt yin, and brocht us through, up to Chubut wi'out a scratch upon the paint.

"A pairfect pilot, though he had naething in the wide world to guide him through they wild stony plains.

"That's how I lost the *Rosebud,* and noo, ma freens, I'll tell you how it was I got Jean, but that was years ago.

"In my youth up in Peterhead I was a sailorman. I went to sea in they North Sea whaling craft, Duff and McAlister's, ye ken. As time went on, I got rated as a harpooner . . . mony's the richt whale I hae fastened into. That was the time when everything was dune by hand. Nane of your harpoon guns, nane of your dynamite, naething but muscle and a keen eye. First strike yer whale, and then pull after him. Talk of yer fox hunts . . . set them up, indeed.

"Jean's father keepit a bit shop in Aberdeen, and we had got acquaint. I cannot richtly mind the way o' it. Her father and her mother were aye against our marryin', for ye ken I had naething but my pay, and that only when I could get a ship. Whiles, too, I drinkit a wee bit. Naething to signify, but then Jean's father was an elder of the kirk, and maist particular.

"Jean was a bonny lassie then, awfu' high-spirited. I used to wonder whiles, if some day when her father had been oot at the kirk, someone hadna slippit in to tak tea with her mither   I ken I'm haverin',

"Weel, we were married, and though we lo'ed each other, we were aye bickerin'. Maistly aboot naething, but ye see, we were both young and spirited. Jean liket admiration, which was natural enough at her age, and I liket speerits, so that ane night, after a word or two, I gied her bit daud or two,[1] maybe it was the speerits, for in the morning when I wakit I felt about for Jean, intending to ask pardon, and feelin' a bit shamed. There was no Jean, and I thocht that she was hidin' just to frichten me.

"I called, but naething, and pittin' on ma clothes searchit the hoose, but there was naebody. She left no message for me, and nane of the neighbours kent anything aboot her.

"She hadna' gone to Aberdeen, and though her father and me searchit up and doon, we got no tidings of her. Sort o' unchancy, just for a day or two. However, there was naething to be done, and in a month or so I sold my furniture and shipped for a long cruise.

"Man, a long cruise it was, three months or more blocked in the ice, and then a month in Greenland trying to get the scurvy out of the ship's company, and so one way or another, about seven months slipped past before we sighted Peterhead. Seven months without a sight of any woman; for, men, they Esquimaux aye gied me a skunner wi' their fur clothes and oily faces, they lookit to be baboons.

"We got in on a Sabbath, and I am just tellin' ye, as soon as I was free, maybe about three o' the afternoon, I fairly ran all the way richt up to Maggie Bauchop's.

"I see the place the noo, up a bit wynd. The town was awfu' quiet, and no one cared to pass too close to the wynd foot in daylight, for fear o' the clash o' tongues. I didna care a rap for that: if there had been a lion in the path, same as once happened to ane o' the prophets—Balaam, I think it was, in the old Book—I wouldna hae stood back a minute if there had been a woman on the other side.

"Weel, I went up to the door, and rappit on it. Maggie came to it, and says she, 'Eh, Christie, is that you?' for she aye kent a customer. A braw, fat woman, Maggie Bauchop was. For years she had followed the old trade, till she had pit awa' a little siller, and started business for hersel'.

"Weel she kent a' the tricks o' it, and still she was a sort of God-fearin' kind o' bitch . . . treated her lassies weel, and didna cheat them about their victuals and their claithes. 'Come in,' she says, 'Christie, my man. Where hae ye come from?'

"I tellt her, and says I, 'Maggie, gie us yer best, I've been seven months at sea.'

" 'Hoot, man,' she says, 'the lassies arena up; we had a fearfu' spate o' drink yestreen, an awfu' lot of ships is in the port. Sit ye doon, Christie. Here's the old Book to ye. Na, na, ye needna look at it like that; there's bonny pictures in it, o' the prophets . . . each wi' his lass, ye ken.'

"When she went out, I looked a little at the book—man, a fine hot one, and then as the time passed I started whistlin' a tune, something I had heard up aboot Hammerfest. The door flees open, and in walks Maggie, looking awfu' mad.

" 'Christie,' she skirls, 'I'll hae na whistlin' in ma hoose, upon the Sabbath day. I canna hae my lassies learned sich ways, so stop it, or get out.'

"Man, I just lauch at her, and I says, 'The lassies, woman; whistlin' can hardly hurt them, considerin' how they live.'

"Maggie just glowered at me, and 'Christie,' she says, 'you and men like ye may defile their bodies; but whilst I live na one shall harm their souls, puir lambies, wi' whistlin' on His day. No, not in my hoose, that's what I'm tellin' ye.'

"I laughed, and said, 'Weel, send us in ane o' your lambies!' and turned to look at a picture of Queen Victoria's Prince Albert picnickin' at Balmoral. When I looked round a girl had come into the room. She was dressed in a striped sort of petticoat and a white jacket, a blouse I think ye ca' the thing, and stood wi' her back to me as she was speaking to Maggie at the door.

"I drew her to me, and was pulling her towards the bed—seven months at sea, ye ken—when we passed by a looking-glass. I saw her face in it, just for a minute, as we were sort o' strugglin'. Ma God, I lowsed her quick enough, and stotterin' backwards sat down upon a chair. 'Twas Jean, who had run off after the bit quarrel that we had more than a year ago. I didna speak, nor did Jean say a word.

"What's that you say?

"Na, na, ma ain wife in sichlike a place, hae ye no delicacy, man? I settled up wi' Maggie, tellin' her Jean was an old friend o' mine, and took her by the hand. We gaed away to Edinburgh, and there I married her again; sort of haversome job; but Jean just wanted it, ye ken. How she came there I never asked her.

"Judge not, the ould Book says, and after all 'twas me gien' her the daud. Weel, weel, things sort of prospered after that. I bought the *Rosebud,* and as ye know piled her up and down at San Julian, some fifteen years ago.

"I never raised ma hand on Jean again. Na, na, I had suffered for it, and Jean if so be she needed ony sort of purification, man, she got it, standing at the wheel o' nichts on the old schooner wi' the spray flyin', on the passage out.

"Not a drop, thankye, Don Hosey. Good nicht, Mr. Mansel; bongsoir, Cossart, I'm just off hame. Jean will be waiting for me."

Note

1. "I hit her once or twice."

Animula Vagula[1]

"You see," the Orchid-hunter said, "this is just how it happened; one of those deaths, that I have seen so many of, here in the wilderness."

He stood upon the steamer's deck, a slight, grave figure, his hair just touched with grey, his flannel Norfolk jacket, which had once been white, toning exactly with his hat and his grey eyes.

At first sight you saw he was an educated man, and when you spoke to him you felt he must have been at some great public school. Yet there was something indefinable about him that spoke of failure. We have no word to express with sympathy the moral qualities of such a man. In Spanish it is all summed up in the expression, "Un infeliz." Unlucky or unhappy, that is, as the world goes; but perhaps fortunate in that interior world to which so many eyes are closed.

Rolling a cigarette between his thin, brown, fever-stricken fingers, he went on: "Yesterday, about two o'clock, in a heat fit to boil your brain, a canoe came slowly up the stream into the settlement. The Indian paddlers walked up the steep bank carrying the body of a man wrapped in a mat. When they had reached the little palm-thatched hut

over which floated the Colombian flag, that marked it as
the official residence of the Captain of the Port, they set
their burden down with the hopeless look that marks the
Indian, as of an orphaned angel.

" 'We found this Mister on the banks,' they said, 'in the
last stage of fever. He spoke but little Christian, and all he
said was, "Doctor, American doctor, Tocatalaima; take me
there."

" 'Here he is, and now who is to pay us for our work? We
have paddled all night long. The canoe we borrowed. Its
owner said that it gains twenty cents a day, and we want
forty cents each, for we have paddled hard to save this
Mister.' Then they stood silent, scratching the mosquito
bites upon their ankles with the other naked foot—a link
between the *Homo sapiens* and some other intermediate
species, long extinct.

"I paid them, giving them something over what they
demanded, and they put on that expression of entire
aloofness which the Indian usually assumes on such occasions, either because thanks stick in his gullet, or he thinks
no thanks are due after a service rendered. They then
went off to drink a glass or two of rum before they started
on their journey home.

"I went to see the body, which lay covered with a sack
under a little shed. Flies buzzed about it, and already a
faint smell of putrefaction reminded one that man is as the
other animals, and that the store of knowledge he piles up
during his life does not avail to stop the course of Nature,
any more than if he had been an orang-outang."

He paused, and, after having lit the cigarette, strolled to
the bulwark of the steamer, which had now got into the
middle of the stream, and then resumed:

"Living as I do in the woods collecting orchids, the
moralising habit grows upon one. It is, as it were, the only
answer that a man has to the aggressiveness of Nature.

"I stood and looked at the man's body in his thin linen

suit which clung to every angle. Beside him was a white pith helmet, and a pair of yellow-tinted spectacles framed in celluloid to look like tortoiseshell, that come down from the States. I never wear them, for I find that everything that you can do without is something gained in life.

"His feet in his white canvas shoes all stained with mud sticking up stiffly and his limp, pallid hands, crossed by the pious Indians, on his chest gave him that helpless look that makes a dead man, as it were, appeal to one for sympathy and protection against the terror, that perhaps for him is not a terror after all; but merely a long rest.

"No one had thought of closing his blue eyes; and as we are but creatures of habit after all, I put my hand into my pocket, and taking out two half-dollar pieces was about to put them on his eyes. Then I remembered that one of them was bad, and you will not believe me, but I could not put the bad piece on his eyes; it looked like cheating him. So I went out and got two little stones, and after washing them put them upon his eyelids, and at least they kept away the flies.

"I don't know how it was, for I believe I am not superstitious, but it seemed to me that those blue eyes, sunk in the livid face to which a three or four days' growth of fair and fluffy beard gave a look of adolescence, looked at me as if they still were searching for the American doctor, who no doubt must have engrossed his last coherent thought as he lay in the canoe.

"As I was looking at him, mopping my face, and now and then killing a mosquito—one gets to do it quite mechanically, although in my case neither mosquitoes nor any other kind of bug annoys me very much—the door was opened and the authorities came in. After the usual salutations—which in Colombia are long and ceremonious, with much unnecessary offering of services, which both sides know will never be required—they said they came to view the body and take the necessary steps; that is, you know, to try to find out who he was and have him buried, for which, the heat at forty centigrade, no time was to be lost.

"A stout Colombian dressed in white clothes, which made his swarthy skin look darker still, giving him, as it were, the air of a black beetle dipped in milk, was the first to arrive. Taking off his flat white cap and gold-rimmed spectacles—articles which in Colombia are certain signs of office—he looked a little at the dead man and said, 'He was an English or American.' Then turning to a soldier who had arrived upon the scene, he asked him where the Indian paddlers were who had brought in the canoe.

"The man went out to look for them, and the hut soon was crowded full of Indians, each with his straw hat held up before his mouth. They gazed upon the body, not sympathetically, nor yet unsympathetically, but with that baffling look that Indians must have put on when first the conquerors appeared amongst them and they found out their arms did not avail them for defence. By means of it they pass through life as relatively unscathed as it is possible for men to do, and by its help they seem to conquer death, taking away its sting, by their indifference.

"None of them said a word, but stared at the dead man, just as they stare at any living stranger, until I felt that the dead eyes would turn in anger at them and shake off the flat stones.

"The man clothed in authority and dusky white re-turned, accompanied by one of those strange out-at-elbows nondescripts who are to be found in every town in South America, and may be best described as 'pen-men'—that is, persons who can read and write and have some far-off dealings with the law. After a whispered conversation the Commissary, turning to the assembled Indians, asked them in a brief voice if they had found the paddlers of the canoe. None of them answered, for a crowd of Indians will never find a spokesman, as each one fears to be made responsible if he says anything at all. A dirty soldier clothed in draggled khaki, barefooted, and with a rusty, sheathless bayonet banging on his thigh, opened the door and said that he knew where they were, but that they both were drunk. The soldier, after a long stare, would have retreated, but the Commissary, turning abruptly to him, said: 'José, go and see that a grave is dug immediately; this Mister has been dead for several hours.' Then looking at the penman, 'Pérez,' he said, 'we will now proceed to the examination of the dead man's papers which the law prescribes.'

"Pérez, who in common with the majority of the uneducated of his race had a great dread of touching a dead body, began to search the pockets of the young man lying so still and angular in the drab-looking suit of white. To put off the dread moment he picked up the pith helmet and, turning out the lining, closely examined it. Then, finding nothing, in his agitation let it fall upon the chest of the dead man. I could have killed him, but said nothing, and we all stood perspiring, with the thermometer at anything you like inside that wretched hut, while Pérez fumbled in the pockets of the dead man's coat.

"It seemed to me as if the unresisting body was somehow being outraged, and that the stiff, attenuated arms would double up and strike the miserable Pérez during his terrifying task. He was so clumsy and so frightened that it seemed an eternity till he produced a case of worn, green leather edged with silver, in which were several brown Havana cigarettes.

"The Commissary gravely remarking, 'We all have vices, great or small, and smoking is but a little frailty,' told Pérez to write down 'Case, 1; cigarettes, 3,' and then to go on with the search. 'The law requires,' he said, 'the identification of all the dead wherever possible.

" 'First, for its proper satisfaction in order that the Code of the Republic should be complied with; and, secondly, for the consolation of the relations, if there are any such, or the friends of the deceased.'

"Throughout the search the Indians stood in a knot, like cattle standing under a tree in summer-time, gathered together, as it were, for mutual protection, without uttering a word. The ragged soldier stared intently; the Commissary occasionally took off his spectacles and wiped them; and the perspiring Pérez slowly brought out a pocket-knife, a box of matches, and a little bottle of quinine. They were all duly noted down, but still no pocket-book, card-case, letter, or any paper with the name of the deceased appeared to justify the search. Pérez would willingly have given up the job; but, urged on by his chief, at last extracted from an interior pocket a letter-case in alligator skin. Much frayed and stained with perspiration, yet its silver tips still showed that it had once been bought at a good shop.

" 'Open it, Pérez, for the law allows one in such cases to take steps that otherwise would be illegal and against that liberal spirit for which we in this Republic are so renowned in the Americas. Then hand me any card or letter that it may contain.'

"Pérez, with the air of one about to execute a formidable duty, opened the case, first slipping off a couple of elastic bands that held the flaps together. From it he took a bundle of American bank-notes wrapped up in tissue-paper, which he handed to his chief. The Commissary took it, and, slipping off the paper, solemnly counted the notes. 'The sum is just two thousand,' he remarked, 'and all in twenties. Pérez, take note of it, and give me any papers that you may have found.' A closer search of every pocket still revealed nothing, and I breathed more freely, as every time the dirty hands of Pérez fumbled about the helpless body I felt a shudder running down my back.

"We all stood baffled, and the Indians slowly filed out without a word, leaving the Commissary with Pérez and myself standing bewildered by the bed. 'Mister,' the Commissary said to me; 'what a strange case! Here are two thousand dollars, which should go to some relation of this unfortunate young man.'

"He counted them again, and, after having given them to his satellite, told him to take them and put them in his safe.

" 'Now, Mister, I will leave you here to keep guard over your countryman whilst I go out to see if they have dug his grave. There is no priest here in the settlement. We only have one come here once a month; and even if there were a priest, the dead man looks as if he had been Protestant.'

"He turned to me, and saying, 'With your permission,' took his hat and left the hut.

"Thus left alone with my compatriot (if he had been one), I took a long look at him, so as to stamp his features in my mind. I had no camera in my possession, and cannot draw—a want that often hinders me in my profession in the description of my rarer plants.

"I looked so long that if the man I saw lying upon that canvas scissor-bed should ever rise again with the same body, I am certain I could recognise him amongst a million men.

"His hands were long and thin, but sunburnt, his feet well shaped, and though his face was sunken and the heat was rapidly discolouring it, the features were well cut. I noted a brown mark upon the cheek, such as in Spanish is called a *lunar,* which gave his delicate and youthful face something of a girlish look, in spite of his moustache. His eyebrows, curiously enough, were dark, and the incipient growth of beard was darker than his hair. His ears were small and set on close to the head—a sign of breeding— and his eyes, although I dared not look at them, having closed them up myself, I knew were blue, and felt they must be staring at me, underneath the stones. In life he might have weighed about ten stone I guess, not more, and must have been well-made and active, though not an athlete, I should think, by the condition of his hands.

"Strangely enough, there seemed to me nothing particularly sad about the look of him. He just was resting after the struggle, that could have lasted in his case but little more than thirty years, and had left slight traces on his face of anything that he had suffered when alive.

"I took the flat stones off his eyes, and was relieved to find they did not open, and after smoothing his fair hair down a little and taking a long look at the fast-altering features I turned away to smoke.

"How long I waited I cannot recollect, but all the details of the hut, the scissor canvas bed on which the body lay, the hooks for hammocks in the mud-and-bamboo walls, the tall brown jar for water, like those that one remembers in the pictures of the *Arabian Nights* in childhood, the drinking gourd beside it, with the two heavy hardwood chairs of ancient Spanish pattern, seated and backed with pieces of raw hide, the wooden table, with the planks showing the marks of the adze that fashioned them, I never shall forget.

"Just at the door there was an old canoe, dug out of a tree-trunk, the gunwale broken and the inside almost filled up with mud. Chickens, of that peculiar mangy-looking breed indigenous to every tropic the whole world over, were feeding at one end of it, and under a low shed thatched with soft palm-leaves stood a miserable horse, whose legs were raw owing to the myriads of horseflies that clustered on them, which no one tried to brush away. Three or four vultures sat on a branch of a dead tree that overhung the hut. Their languid eyes appeared to me to pierce the palm-tree roof as they sat on, just as a shark follows a boat in which there is a dead man, waiting patiently.

"Over the bluff, on which the wretched little Ranchería straggled till it was swallowed up in the primeval woods, flowed the great river, majestic, yellow, alligator-haunted, bearing upon its ample bosom thousands of floating masses of green vegetation which had slipped into the flood.

"How long I sat I do not know, and I shall never know, but probably not above half an hour. Still, in that time I saw the life of the young man who lay before me. His voyage out; the first sight of the tropics; the landing into that strange world of swarthy-coloured men, dank vegetation, thick, close atmosphere, the metallic hum of insects, and the peculiar smell of a hot country—things which we see and hear once in our lives, and but once only, for custom dulls the senses, and we see nothing more. Then the letters home, simple and child-like in regard to life, but shrewd and penetrating as regards business, after the fashion of the Northern European or his descendants in the United States.

I saw him pass his first night in the bare tropical hotel, under a mosquito-curtain, and then wake up to all the glory of the New World he had discovered for himself, as truly as Columbus did when he had landed upon Guanahani on that eventful Sunday morning and unfurled the flag of Spain. I heard him falter out his first few words in broken Spanish, and saw him take his first walk, either by the harbour, thronged with its unfamiliar-looking boats piled up with fish and fruits unknown in Europe, or through the evil-smelling, badly-paved alleys in the town.

"The voyage up the river, with the first breath of the asphyxiating heat; the flocks of parrots; the alligators, so like dead logs, all basking in the sun; the stopping in the middle of the night for wood beside some landing-place cut in the jungle, where men, naked but for a cloth tied round their loins, ran up a plank and dumped their load down with a half-sigh, half-yell—I saw and heard it all. Then came the arrival at the mine or rubber station, the long and weary days, the fevers, the rare letters, and the cherished newspapers from home—those, too, I knew of, for I had waited for them often in my youth.

"Most of all, as I looked on him and saw his altering features, I thought of his snug home in Massachusetts or Northumberland, where his relations looked for letters on thin paper, with the strange postmarks, which would never come again. How they would wonder in his home, and here was I looking at the features that they would give the world to see, but impotent to help."

He stopped, and, walking to the bulwarks, looked up the river, and said: "In half an hour we shall arrive at San Fulgencio. . . . They came and fetched the body, and wrapped it in a white cotton sheet—for which I paid—and we set off, followed by the few storekeepers, two Syrians and a Portuguese, and a small crowd of Indians.

"There was no cemetery—that is to say, not one of those Colombian cemeteries fenced with barbed wire, in which the plastered gateway looks like an afterthought, and where the iron crosses blistering in the sun look drearier than any other crosses in the world.

"Under a clump of Guáduas—that is the name they give to the bamboo—there was a plot of ground fenced in with canes. In it the grave was dug amongst some others, on which a mass of grass and weeds was growing, as if it wished to blot them out from memory as soon as possible.

"A little wooden cross or two, with pieces of white paper periodically renewed, affirmed that Resurreción Venegas or Exaltación Machuca reposed beneath the weeds.

"The grave looked hard and uninviting, and as we laid him in it, lowering him with a rope made of lianas, two or three macaws flew past, uttering a raucous cry.

"The Commissary had put on a black suit of clothes, and Pérez had a rusty band of cloth pinned round his arm. The Syrians and the Portuguese took off their hats, and as there was no priest the Commissary mumbled some formula; and I, advancing to the grave, took a last look at the white sheet which showed the angles of the frail body underneath it, but for the life of me I could not say a word, except 'Good-bye.'

"When the Indians had filled in the earth we all walked back towards the settlement perspiring. I took a glass of rum with them, just for civility . . . I think I paid for it . . . and then I gathered up my traps and sat and waited under a big Bongo-tree until the steamer came along."

A silence fell upon us all, as sitting in our rocking-chairs upon the high deck of the stern-wheel steamer, we mused instinctively upon the fate of the unknown young Englishman, or American. The engineer from Oregon, the Texan cow-puncher going to look at cattle in the Llanos de Bolívar, and all the various waifs and strays that get together upon a voyage up the Magdalena, no doubt each thought he might have died, just as the unknown man had died, out in the wilderness.

No one said anything, until the orchid-hunter, as the steamer drew into the bank, said: "That is San Fulgencio. I go ashore here. If any of you fellows ever find out who the chap was, send us a line to Barranquilla; that's where my wife lives.

"I am just off to the Chocó, a three or four months' job. . . . Fever?—oh, yes, sometimes, of course, but I think nothing of it. . . . Quinine?—thanks, yes, I've got it. . . . I don't believe in it a great deal. . . . Mosquitoes? . . . no, they do not worry me. A gun? . . . well, no, I never carry arms . . . thanks all the same. . . . I was sorry, too, for that poor fellow; but, after all, it is the death I'd like to die myself. . . . No, thanks, I don't care for spirits. . . . Good-bye to all of you."

We waved our hands and crowded on the steamer's side, and watched him walking up the bank to where a little group of Indians stood holding a bullock with a pack upon its back.

They took his scanty property and, after tying it upon the ox, set off at a slow walk along a little path towards the jungle, with the grey figure of our late companion walking quietly along, a pace or two behind.

Note

1. A poem by the Emperor Hadrian begins:

> Animula vagula blandula,
> Hospes comesque corporis,
> Quae nunc abibis in loca. . . .
> (Pleasant and wandering little soul,
> Guest and partner of the body,
> Where will you go to now?)

The Stationmaster's Horse

After the long war in Paraguay, the little railway built by the tyrant López, that ran from Asunción to Paraguari, only some thirty miles, fell into a semi-ruinous condition.

It still performed a journey on alternate days, and ran, or rather staggered, along on a rough track, almost unballasted. Sleepers had been taken out for firewood, by the country people here and there, or had decayed and never been replaced. The line was quite unfenced, and now and then a bullock strayed upon it and was run down or sometimes was found sleeping on the track. Then the train stopped, if the engine-driver saw the animal in time. He blew his whistle loudly, the passengers all started, and if the bullock refused to move, got down and stoned it off the line. The bridges luckily were few, and were constructed of the hard imperishable woods so plentiful in Paraguay. They had no railings, and when, after the downpours of the tropics, the streams they crossed were flooded, the water lapped up and covered them to the depth of several inches, so that the train appeared to roll upon the waters, and gave the passengers an experience they were not likely to forget. The engine-driver kept his

eyes fixed firmly on a tree or any other object on the bank,
just as a man crossing a flooded stream on horseback dares
not look down upon the rushing waters, but stares in front
of him, above his horse's head. Overhead bridges fortu-
nately did not exist, and there was but a single cutting in
the thirty miles. It filled with water in the rains, and now
and then delayed the trains a day or two, but no one
minded, for time was what the people had the most of on
their hands, and certainly they were not niggardly in the
disposal of it.

The engines that burned wood achieved a maximum of
ten miles an hour, but again no one minded, for that was
greater than the speed of the bullock carts to which they
had been accustomed all their lives.

Thus they looked on the railway as a marvel, and spoke
of it as a sign of progress that ennobled man and made
him truly only a little lower than the angels and the best
beloved creation of the Deity.

Shares, dividends, balance sheets, and all the rest of the
mysterious processes without which no railway in these
more favoured times can run a yard, were never heard of,
for the line was run by Government, who paid the salaries
of the engine-drivers, who were all foreigners, when they
had any cash in hand. When there was none, the officials,
who had all married Paraguayan women, were left dependent on their efforts for a meal.

The telegraph, with the wires sagging like the lianas
sagged from tree to tree in the great woods through which
the greater portion of the line was built, was seldom in
good order, so that as it stopped at the rail-head of the
line, the better plan was to entrust a letter to the guard or
engine-driver.

Certainly that little line through the primeval forest,
with now and then breaks of open plain, dotted here and
there with the dwarf scrubby palms called yatais, was one

of the most curious and interesting the world has ever known. The trains in general started an hour or two behind the time that they were supposed to start, picking up passengers like an old-time omnibus. Men standing at the corner of a wood waved coats or handkerchiefs, or in some cases a green palm leaf, to the engine-driver. He generally slowed down his impetuous career to about three miles an hour, and then the signaller, running alongside, was pulled up by a score of willing hands stretched out to him. In the case when the signaller had women with him, or a package too heavy to be thrown upon a truck in motion, the train would stop, the people scramble up, and haul their package up after them. Sometimes a man on horseback, urging his horse up to the train, with shouts, and blows of his flat-lashed *rebenque* that sounded much severer than they really were, and keeping up a ceaseless drumming of his bare heels upon its flanks, would hand a letter or a little packet to the engine-driver or to some travelling friend. At times the train appeared to stop for no apparent reason, as nobody appeared out of the forest, either to pass the time of day or to enquire ths news. Upon inclines, active young men sprinted behind the train until they caught up the last wagons; then, encouraged by the riders—for to call them "passengers" would be an unnecessary euphemism—and placing a brown hand upon the moving truck, they vaulted inboard and lay breathless for a minute, perspiring plentifully. At places such as Luque, Itá and Ipacaray, the little townships through which the harbinger of progress ran, the stops were lengthy.

Women in long white sleeveless smocks (their only garment) went about selling *chipá*—the Paraguayan bread of mandioca flour, flavoured with cheese, as indigestible as an old-fashioned Pitcaithly bannock—pieces of sugarcane, oranges and bananas, rough lumps of dark brown sugar, done up in plantain leaves, and tasting of the lye used in

their manufacture, with other delicacies called in Spanish
"fruits of the country."[1] The sun poured down upon the
platform, crowded with women, for men were very scarce
in Paraguay in those days. They kept up a perpetual shrill
chattering in Guaraní; occasionally in broken Spanish,
plentifully interlarded with interjections, such as *Baié pico,
Iponaité, Añariu,* in their more familiar tongue. Outside the
station the donkeys on which the women had brought
their merchandise nibbled the waving grass or chased one
another in the sand. A scraggy horse or two, looking half
starved and saddled with a miserable old native saddle, the
stirrups often a mere knot of hide to be held by the naked
toes, nodded in the fierce sun with his feet hobbled or
fastened to a post. After a longer or a shorter interval, the
stationmaster, generally well-dressed in white, his head
crowned with an official semi-military cap, his bare feet
shoved into carpincho leather slippers down at heel, and
smoking a cigar, would appear upon the platform, elbow
his way amongst the crowd of women, pinching them and
addressing salacious compliments to those he deemed
attractive, till he reached the guard or engine-driver, gos-
sip a little with him, and signal to a female porter to ring
the starting bell. This she did with a perfunctory air. The
engine-driver sounded his whistle shrilly, and the train, in
a long series of jerks, as if protesting, bumped off from the
platform in a cloud of dust.

Difference of classes may have existed, but only
theoretically, like the rights of man, equality, liberty, or
any of the other mendacious bywords that mankind loves
to write large and disregard. No matter what the
passenger unused to Paraguay paid for his ticket, the
carriage was at once invaded by the other travellers,
smoking and talking volubly and spitting so profusely that
it was evident that no matter what diseases Paraguay was
subject to, consumption had no place amongst them.

The jolting was terrific, the heat infernal, and the whole

train crowded with people, who sat in open trucks, upon the tops of carriages, on footboards, or on anything that would contain them, smoking and chattering, and in their white clothes as the train slowly jolted onwards, looking like a swarm of butterflies. Certainly its progress was not speedy, but as a general rule it reached its destination, though hours behind its time.

Having to write one day from the railhead at Paraguari to Asunción, only some thirty miles away, as the train started by a miracle at the hour that it was advertised to start, I missed it, and as the trains ran only on alternate days, the telegraph was not in working order, and no one happened to be going to the capital, someone advised me to borrow a good horse and overtake the train at some of its innumerable stoppages.

The stationmaster lent me his Zebruno, that is a cream colour, so dark as to be almost brown, with a black mane and tail, a colour that in the Argentine is much esteemed as a sure sign of a good constitution in a horse, and staying power.

He proved a little hard to mount, for he was full of corn and seldom ridden, and more than a little hard to stay upon his back for the first few minutes, a little scary, but high-couraged and as sure-footed as a mule.

I overtook the train some ten miles down the line, at a small station—Itá, if I remember rightly—after a wild ride, on a red sandy road, mostly through forest, close to the railway line, so that it was impossible to lose the track, although I did not know a yard of it.

Now and then it emerged upon the plain, and then, taking the Zebruno by the head, who by this time was settling down a little, I touched him with the spur. He answered, snorting, with a bound, and then I made good time.

I gave the letter to the engine-driver, who put it carefully into the pocket of his belt, crumpling it up so that it looked like a dead locust. Then wishing me good luck on my ride home, for night was falling, the road was almost uninhabited, tigers abounded and there was always a chance of meeting with "bad people" (*"mala gente"*), he cursed the country heartily, lit a cigar, spat with precision on to the track, released his lever and slid into the night.

The cream colour, who had got his second wind and rested, reared as the hind-lights passed him, and as I wheeled him, struck into a steady gallop that, as the phrase goes, "soon eats up the leagues."

A light breeze raised his mane a little and set the palm trees rustling, fireflies came out and lit the clumps of the wild orange trees, looking like spirits of disembodied butterflies as they flitted to and fro. Occasionally we—that is the cream colour and myself—had a slight difference of opinion at the crossing of a stream, when the musky scent of an unseen alligator or an ominous rustling in the thickets startled him.

As we cantered into Paraguari, he was still pulling at his bit, and nearly terminated my career in this vale of tears by a wild rush he made to get into his shed, that was too low to let a man pass underneath on horseback. I thanked the stationmaster for his horse, unsaddled him, emptied a tin mug of water over his sweating back, and threw him down a bundle of fresh Pindó leaves to keep him occupied till he was ready for his maize.

Then I strolled into the station café, where Exaltación Medina, João Ferreira, and, I think, Enrique Clerici were playing billiards, whilst they waited for me.

Note

1. *Frutos del país.* [C. G.]

Part IV

Caudal

Conclusion

In his lifetime, when he was a celebrity commemorated in the pages of Shaw, Conrad and Wells, Graham received unintentional or benevolently-intended denigration from those who found much to admire in him. This was at the time when Galsworthy, Epstein and others established the myth that he was a modern Don Quixote: a subtly denigratory myth, for it implied that he was an anachronism, a chivalric figure in the wrong age. The political polemics in Part II of this book may have suggested the contrary: that in his insights he was proleptic rather than anachronistic, and that in his onslaughts against the injustices of nation to nation, class to class and sex to sex he was indeed tilting at giants rather than at windmills.

Those few people who know his works today can still subject him to another form of denigration, by saying that in his achievements he was always a second-rater. He had lively political views, but his intelligence varied between that of a hare-brained Hotspur and an astute Prince Hal, and he was never a powerful guiding-force. For his literary works, he may have had a high reputation in his day, but now his sketches will often seem slight and amateurish alongside tales by Lawrence, Conrad or Joyce. In his travels, too, he had his adventures, but they never resulted in the achievements of a Burton or a Doughty. Typically, when Graham set out for the forbidden city of Tarudant, he failed to reach his objective; just as his struggle to redeem from debt the ancestral home, Gartmore, was doomed to failure, and just as his attempts to gain wealth by cattle-ranching, gold-mining and trade concessions were all abortive.

What this view ignores is the quality of endeavour within an amazingly wide range of activities: the exuberant energy of Graham's protean life. It is, finally, as a vivid personality that he deserves to be recalled; and the selections in this book will have done their job if they draw attention to a proud, fallible and humane individual who, in the words of his monument at Dumbarton, was a Master of Life.

Bibliography

When the place of publication is not stated, the place is London.

1. Books by Cunninghame Graham

Notes on the District of Menteith. Black, 1895.
Father Archangel of Scotland. (Written jointly with his wife.) Black, 1896.
Mogreb-el-Acksa. Heinemann, 1898.
The Ipané. Fisher Unwin, 1899.
Thirteen Stories. Heinemann, 1900.
A Vanished Arcadia. Heinemann, 1901.
Success. Duckworth, 1902.
Hernando de Soto. Heinemann, 1903.
Progress. Duckworth, 1905.
His People. Duckworth, 1906.
Faith. Duckworth, 1909.
Hope. Duckworth, 1910.
Charity. Duckworth, 1912.
A Hatchment. Duckworth, 1913.
Bernal Díaz del Castillo. Nash, 1915.
Brought Forward. Duckworth, 1916.
A Brazilian Mystic. Heinemann, 1920.

Cartagena and the Banks of the Sinú. Heinemann, 1920.
The Conquest of New Granada. Heinemann, 1922.
The Conquest of the River Plate. Heinemann, 1924.
Doughty Deeds. Heinemann, 1925.
Pedro de Valdivia. Heinemann, 1926.
Redeemed. Heinemann, 1927.
José Antonio Páez. Heinemann, 1929.
The Horses of the Conquest. Heinemann, 1930.
Writ in Sand. Heinemann, 1932.
Portrait of a Dictator. Heinemann, 1933.
Mirages. Heinemann, 1936.

2. Pamphlets and Booklets

The Nail and Chainmakers. (Graham was one of three con-
tributors, the others being J. L. Mahon and C. A. V. Cony-
beare.) London Press Agency, 1889.
Economic Evolution. Aberdeen: Leatham; London: Reeves, 1891.
The Imperial Kailyard. Twentieth Century Press, 1896.
Aurora la Cujiñi. Smithers, 1898.
The Dream of the Magi. Heinemann, 1923.
Inveni Portam: Joseph Conrad. Cleveland: Rowfant Club, 1924.
Bibi. Heinemann, 1929.
With the North-West Wind. Berkeley Heights, N. J.: Oriole Press,
1934.
Two Letters on an Albatross. (One is by Graham, the other by W. H.
Hudson.) Hanover, N. H.: Westholm, 1955.
Three Fugitive Pieces. Hanover, N. H.:Westholm, 1960.

3. Selections from material which had previously appeared in book form

Scottish Stories. Duckworth, 1914.
Thirty Tales and Sketches. Duckworth, 1929.
Rodeo. Heinemann, 1936.
The Essential R. B. Cunninghame Graham. Cape, 1952.
Selected Short Stories. Madrid: Alhambra, 1959.
The South American Sketches. Norman: Oklahoma, 1978.

4. Translations

Gustavo Barroso. *Mapirunga*. Heinemann, 1924.
The Madonna of the Sea. (A version of Santiago Rusiñol's Catalán text, *La Verge del Mar*.) Unpublished, but performed at Norwich in 1958.

5. Works by other authors with prefaces or introductions by Graham

J. L. Mahon. *A Labour Programme*. London Press Agency, 1888.
Gabriela Cunninghame Graham. *Santa Teresa*. Black, 1894, and Nash, 1907. (Two different prefaces.)
Anonymous [William Stirling]. *The Canon*. Mathews, 1897.
S. Pérez Triana. *Down the Orinoco in a Canoe*. Heinemann, 1902. (As *De Bogota al Atlántico*: Madrid, 1905.)
M. Aflalo. *The Truth about Morocco*. Lane, 1904.
I. A. Taylor. *Revolutionary Types*. Duckworth, 1904.
C. Rudy. *Companions in the Sierra*. Lane, 1907.
Gabriela Cunninghame Graham. *The Christ of Toro*. Nash, 1908.
Gabriela Cunninghame Graham. *Rhymes from a World Unknown*. Privately printed, 1908.
Martin Hume. *True Stories of the Past*. Nash, 1910.
Martin Hume. *Queens of Old Spain*. Richards, 1911.
C. Rosher. *Light for John Bull on the Moroccan Question*. Henderson, 1911.
Emily, Shareefa of Wazan. *My Life Story*. Arnold, 1911.
W. Shaw-Sparrow. *John Lavery and His Work*. Kegan Paul, 1912.
W. H. Koebel. *In Jesuit Land*. S. Paul, 1912.
M. Radclyffe Hall. *Songs of Three Counties*. Chapman & Hall, 1913.
A. C. Rickett. *William Morris*. Jenkins, 1913.
Miguel de Cervantes Saavedra. *Rinconete and Cortadillo*. Translated by M. J. Lorente. Boston: Four Seas, 1917.
Salvador de Madariaga. *Manojo de Poesías Inglesas*. Nutt, 1919.
C. H. Prodgers. *Adventures in Bolivia*. Lane, 1922.
F. W. Up de Graff. *Head-Hunters of the Amazon*. Jenkins, 1922 (with "1923" imprint). (As *Cazadores de cabezas del Amazonas*: Madrid: Espasa-Calpe, 1928).
W. H. Hudson. *Birds of La Plata*. Dent, 1923.

Morley Roberts. *The Western Avernus*. Dent, 1924.

Charles Simpson. *El Rodeo*. Lane, 1924.

Gustavo Barroso. *Mapirunga*. Heinemann, 1924.

Wilfranc Hubbard. *Orvieto Dust*. Constable, 1925.

A. C. G. Hastings. *Nigerian Days*. Lane, 1925.

J. M. Dowsett. *Big Game and Big Life*. Bale, 1925.

Joseph Conrad. *Tales of Hearsay*. Fisher Unwin, 1925.

H. de Maupassant. *Tales from Maupassant*. Nash & Grayson, 1926.

A. Gudsow. *The Princess Biaslantt*. Heinemann, 1926.

W. H. Hudson. *La tierra purpúrea*. Madrid: Sociedad General Española de Librería, 1928.

J. M. Dowsett. *The Spanish Bull Ring*. Bale, 1928.

H. Hope-Nicholson, ed. *The Mindes Delight*. Richards, 1928.

R. N. Green-Armytage, ed. *The Book of Martin Harvey*. Walker, 1930.

T. D. Lauder. *The Wolfe of Badenoch*. Stirling: Mackay, 1930.

John A. Fleming. *Flemish Influences in Britain*. Glasgow: Jackson & Wylie, 1930.

Rafael de Nogales. *Memoirs of a Soldier of Fortune*. Wright & Brown, 1931.

W. H. Hudson. *Far Away and Long Ago*. Dent, 1931.

J. Ressich. *Gallop!* Benn, 1932.

Robert Kirk. *The Secret Commonwealth of Elves, Fauns and Fairies*. Stirling: Mackay, 1933.

J. A. Stewart. *Inchmahome and the Lake of Menteith*. Edinburgh: Privately printed, 1933.

A. F. Tschiffely. *Southern Cross to Pole Star: Tschiffely's Ride*. Heinemann, 1933. (As *Tschiffely's Ride:* New York: Simon & Schuster, 1933; Heinemann, 1934; Hodder & Stoughton, 1952.)

A. F. Tschiffely. *The Tale of Two Horses*. Heinemann, 1934. (As *Mancha y Gato:* Buenos Aires: Emecé, 1944.)

Joseph Conrad. *Lord Jim*. Dent, 1935.

S. L. Bensusan. *Annals of Maychester*. Routledge, 1936.

Cunninghame Graham also provided introductions for the catalogues of the following art exhibitions: John Lavery (London: Leicester Galleries, 1904); Muirhead Bone (London: Colnaghi Galleries, 1930); C. Bernaldo de Quirós (London: Tate

Gallery, 1931); Edward Wolfe (London: Cooling Galleries, 1932); Jacomb Hood (London, 1934).

6. Books about Cunninghame Graham.

H. F. West. *A Modern Conquistador.* Cranley and Day, 1932.
A. F. Tschiffely. *Don Roberto.* Heinemann, 1937. *Tornado Cavalier.* Harrap, 1955.
Hugh MacDiarmid. *Cunninghame Graham: A Centenary Study.* Glasgow: Caledonian Press, 1952.
R. E. Haymaker. *Prince-Errant and Evocator of Horizons.* Kingsport, Tenn.: Privately printed, 1967.
Cedric Watts and Laurence Davies. *Cunninghame Graham: A Critical Biography.* Cambridge, 1979.

7. Articles or sections on Cunninghame Graham: A selection

G.B. Shaw. "Notes to *Captain Brassbound's Conversion*" in *Three Plays for Puritans.* Richards, 1901.
Frank Harris. *Contemporary Portraits (3rd Series).* New York: Harris, 1920.
Arthur Symons. *Notes on Joseph Conrad.* Myers, 1925.
D. H. Lawrence. "*Pedro de Valdivia . . .*" *The Calendar,* vol. 3 (1927).
Edward Garnett. Introduction to Graham's *Thirty Tales and Sketches.* Duckworth, 1929.
John Galsworthy. *Forsytes, Pendyces and Others.* Heinemann, 1935.
R. W. Stallman. "Robert Cunninghame Graham's South American Sketches." *Hispania,* vol. 28 (1945).
Cedric Watts. "R. B. Cunninghame Graham (1852-1936): A List of His Contributions to Periodicals." *The Bibliotheck,* vol. 4 (1965); supplemented by John Walker in *The Bibliotheck,* vol. 7 (1974).
James Steel Smith. "R. B. Cunninghame Graham as a Writer of Short Fiction." *English Literature in Transition,* vol. 12 (1969).
Laurence Davies. "Cunninghame Graham's South American Sketches." *Comparative Literature Studies,* vol. 9 (1972).

Glossary

Adobe: brick made of sun-dried mud
aguape: water plant
ahuehuete: cypress
alameda: park

bask (Scots): sharp
bayou: sluggish stream or swampy area
bing: heap
birlin' (birling) at the clairet: carousing with claret wine
bolsón: lagoon
boss (Scots): hollow, empty
braw: fine

cacoethes: itch
cacoethes operandi: an itch to work
calkin: pointed piece on a horseshoe, to prevent slipping
Campo Santo (camposanto): cemetery
capataz: foreman, superintendent
carl: niggardly, churlish fellow
chaparejos: chaps, leather leggings
Corpo del Bambin: By the body of the infant Jesus!
la cuesta de los fierros: the hillside of iron
cwt. (hundredweight): 50.8 kilograms

dang the haricles oot: knocked out the contents
daud: a blow or thump
daunder: saunter
défroque: outfit of old clothes
divette: variety actress or singer
dour thrawn body: obstinate and perverse fellow
dreich: dreary
duar: encampment or tent village

encrucijada: crossroad

fecht: fight
feck: number, quantity
forby: besides
fou: drunk

game yin: brave one
ganaker (guanaco): wild llama
gash (Scots): ghastly
girned: grinned or snarled
gobierno: government
grat sair: cried bitterly
greeting (Scots): weeping

hacienda: estate or ranch
haik: robe
hegira: flight or escape
heughin' (heughing): digging, hoeing
hurl (Scots): journey in a wheeled vehicle

istle: fiber obtained from plants

jacal: rough Indian shelter
Jawi: Javanese

kasbah: castle or fortress

keelin' (keeling): marking with ruddle
ken: know
kist: coffin

lepero: wretch, rogue

mecate: rope or cord
mehari: dromedary
mescal: the peyote cactus
mesón: inn
metate: flat stone
mezquite (mesquite): leguminous tree or shrub
muckle: much
Mueran los Indios salvajes!: Death to the wild Indians!
muezzin: Muslim who calls men to prayer

neeps: turnips

painter (U.S.): cougar
palenque: stockade or hitching post
pampero: violent wind of the pampas
pantomimas, que salen en las fiestas: clowns, who perform at
    the festivals
per Bacco!: by Bacchus!
poblana, poblano: native
puckle: few
pulpería: pampas store or tavern
pulque: drink made from fermented maguey juice

razzias: pillaging incursions
rebenque: rawhide whip
rekass: runner, messenger
resaca: dried or marshy course of a stream
Riding: region

shauchle: stiff, worn-out

shilpit: sickly-looking
Shinghiti: man of Shinghit, in the Western Sahara
siba: revolt
skilly: thin gruel
skunner: feeling of disgust
stan' o' black: formal black suit
stour: dust
su Gigia: up you go, Gigia
suddra zariba: stockade, thorn-hedge fortification
summum bonum: the chief good
syne: then

tak fuff: become angry
tatties: potatoes
thrawn: perverse, cross-grained
tierra caliente: hot land
tierra fría: cold land
tilt: awning
tortillers (tortillas): cornmeal pancakes

Viva los valientes!: Long live the brave!

wynd· lane, alley

yin: one (individual, person)

Index

211